WYLIE ENDER'S
SURVIVE
CRASH

EPIC
Escape

An Imprint of EPIC Press
EPICPRESS.COM

Crash
Survive

Written by Wylie Ender

Copyright © 2018 by Abdo Consulting Group, Inc.

Published by EPIC Press™
PO Box 398166
Minneapolis, MN 55439

Cover design by Christina Doffing
Images for cover art obtained from iStockPhoto.com
Edited by Rue Moran

LIBRARY OF CONGRESS CATALOGING-IN-PUBLICATION DATA
Names: Ender, Wylie, author.
Title: Crash / by Wylie Ender.
Description: Minneapolis, MN : EPIC Press, 2018. | Series: Survive
Summary: After losing an important competition, Gloria thinks she's hit rock bottom, but a
   plane crash proves her wrong. She and many others are left stranded in the middle of the
   Arizona desert. Gloria soon realizes that technical ability doesn't help in one of the world's
   harshest climates.
Identifiers: LCCN 2016962621 | ISBN 9781680767308 (lib. bdg.) |
   ISBN 9781680767865 (ebook)
Subjects: LCSH: Disasters—Fiction. | Wilderness survival—Fiction. | Adventure and
   adventurers—Fiction. | Survival—Fiction. | Young adult fiction.
Classification: DDC [Fic]—dc23
LC record available at http://lccn.loc.gov/2016962621

"When you come to the end of your rope, tie a knot and hang on."
—*Franklin D. Roosevelt*

CHAPTER 1

"This is awesome," my music teacher, Mr. Wilkins, says. Mr. Wilkins is always saying that. This is awesome, that is awesome, look how awesome everything is. He has low expectations. "Look, Gloria, so much room!"

This time, I reluctantly agree with him, though I'd never tell Mr. Wilkins that. The small plane's seats are blue leather with built-in screens and there's a good amount of space between the seatback and my knees. My violin has enough room to be stowed under my seat, which I'd normally be thankful for since it's pretty delicate even in its case. But right now I really don't want my instrument anywhere near me.

Mr. Wilkins isn't saying how awesome the competition was, because I lost—badly. And now both he and I have to fly back to California to face my parents. As classical musicians, I wonder how they feel about having such a talentless daughter. Do they think they got the wrong baby at the hospital? I know I do.

I'm in a bad mood as we make our way to the back at the flight attendant's direction. I sink into my aisle seat without waiting for Mr. Wilkins to slide in, forcing him to step over me to get to his window seat. It's not nice of me and he sighs as he hops over my sweatpants-covered legs.

I shove my violin under the seat in front of me, then flop back and cross my arms over my stomach as if trying to alleviate the sick feeling in my gut.

"What do you play?"

I look across the aisle at the question and stare blankly at the boy sitting there. He's a couple of years older than me with light brown eyes, clear skin, and floppy brown hair. He looks like an athlete and the jersey he's wearing confirms it. He's really, really cute and I'm suddenly conscious that I haven't brushed my hair since last night and that I'm in sweatpants.

"Violin," I mutter. Normally I wouldn't be so rude, but I do *not* feel like talking to anyone right now.

I can see him smile brightly out of the corner of my eye. "You any good?" he asks.

My mood sours even further and I turn my whole body away, toward Mr. Wilkins, showing the boy my back. "No."

"Oh," the boy says. I can hear the frown in his voice and then the sound of him turning away, disappointed. Good. Everyone should be disappointed in me.

"He thinks you're cute," Mr. Wilkins whispers. His thick eyebrows bob up and down. "He wanted to talk to you."

"Don't care," I say and hunch down in my seat.

Mr. Wilkins is silent for a long moment and, naively, I think that he's taken a hint and is leaving me alone. My hopes are dashed when he reaches over and pats my knee. "You doing okay?"

The concern in his voice makes my throat ache and heat rise behind my eyes. I want to tell him that, no, I'm not okay. I don't want to fly back to California empty-handed—again. I don't want Mr. Wilkins to have to try to explain why I didn't win—again. I don't want him to have to defend his tutoring to my parents like it was his fault that I lost. It's embarrassing.

"I'm fine," I snap, turning away from Mr. Wilkins. I draw my hood up for good measure, blocking out the sight of Mr. Wilkins and the boy. I just want to be left alone.

The P.A. system crackles overhead as it turns on. "Good morning, passengers. Welcome aboard Flight 302 from Dallas to Burbank. Please direct your attention to your flight attendants as they walk you through our safety procedures."

I ignore the demonstration, staring at the black screen in front of me like it'll burst into flames. That's why I don't notice the flight attendant until he's right next to me.

"Welcome aboard," he says cheerfully. He puts one hand on the back of my seat and leans on it, pushing it back. "My name is Henry. You two are in an emergency exit row and there are certain requirements we need to go through before we take off. Are you both willing and able to help in the case of an emergency?"

"Yes," Mr. Wilkins says. He leans forward so he can look around me at Henry. "I'm CPR certified."

Henry smiles politely but it doesn't reach his eyes. "That's great. Now, I have to ask, how old are you, young lady?"

With his curly hair, bright green eyes, and round cheeks, Henry looks like a lot of seniors at my high school so I don't know how I feel about being called "young lady" by him.

"Fourteen," I tell him.

Henry's face pinches apologetically. "Ooh, I'm sorry but you need to be at least fifteen to sit in an exit row. I'm going to have to switch you with another passenger."

"She's with me," Mr. Wilkins says. "Can't you overlook it? She'll be fifteen in two months."

"I'm sorry," Henry says and actually manages to sound it, "but rules are rules."

Mr. Wilkins looks like he's about to protest again or even make a scene. Before he can, I lurch out of my seat, forcing Henry to step back, and snatch my violin out from the seat. "It's fine, Mr. Wilkins."

"If you're sure," he says doubtfully. "I'll be right back here if you need anything."

"Thanks," I say. What does he think I would need him for in the next few hours? We're on a plane.

Henry leads me toward the front of the airplane.

I hug my violin to my chest so I don't accidentally hit any other passengers with it and accidentally make eye contact with a white-haired woman in a large, purple hat. She scowls at me and I instinctively mirror her before looking away. Some people are just rude.

I stow my violin under my new seat, taking in my seat companion from the corner of my eye. She probably wouldn't notice if I did look at her head-on, since her eyes are tightly shut. I can hear the bass coming from the headphones nearly hidden in her thick, black hair.

"Let me know if you need anything," Henry says. He watches me buckle my seat belt and smiles brightly. "Enjoy the flight!"

I pull out my own iPod and headphones, mimicking the girl next to me, and settle back for takeoff.

I've been on dozens of planes, some even smaller than this one. I'd guess there are about thirty people on this plane, but I've been in one where four people were a tight fit. My parents get flown all around the country to perform. They used to take me before I got old enough to be left home alone. This competition was the first time I'd ever left them home while I traveled.

The plane's take-off is smooth, with little turbulence as we gain altitude. I wish I was by the window so I could see Dallas fall away from us and disappear. I settle back for the long flight.

I'm just dozing off when the girl next to me taps me on the shoulder.

"Bathroom," she says, voice croaky from sleep. She clears her throat. "Sorry."

I glance up at the "fasten seat belt" sign, which is decidedly still lit. But hey, what am I, a cop? I get up for the second she needs to slide by and re-buckle before Henry can come over with his disapproving look. The girl disappears into the bathroom at the front of the plane before Henry can catch her.

I take the opportunity to lean over the other seat and flip open the window. A flash of light catches my eye from below and I frown as I realize that it's lightning. I know that lightning isn't really that big of a deal in a plane anymore but it's still unsettling to see.

"I'm back, move quick," the girl says. She bounces on her heels and shoots a quick glance at Henry, who's preparing drinks at the front of the plane. I let her by and she drops into her seat with a *thud*. "Thanks. That guy is a total mother hen. He's been tailing me since we boarded because I'm a single flier."

Being a single flier meant that she was probably about fourteen, like me. She didn't look it with her eyes outlined in thick kohl and her lips painted a fire-engine red. Knowing we were the same age, though, made me relax a little.

"I'm Gloria," I say. I don't reach for her hand, partly because of the awkward angle and partly because she doesn't seem like the kind of person who shakes hands. "My babysitter's in the back."

"Call me Max," she says. She looks back as if she could spot Mr. Wilkins. "Babysitter?"

"He's my music tutor, technically, but all he really does is hover," I explain. "He picks me up from school when my parents are out of town."

"He doesn't teach you music?" she asks.

She means it as a joke but the humiliation of sitting onstage is still fresh so I answer seriously. My terrible performance had been because of me, not because of Mr. Wilkins. "I think he tries but there's, um, limited success."

"Limited success" is a phrase the nicest judge scribbled on my scoring sheet. It basically means "not good."

I abruptly switch topics, not wanting to talk about music anymore. "How long have we been in the air?"

Max consults her MP3 player. "Almost two hours. Better question: how long is this flight?"

"Four—" I start to say when there's a huge lurch. My stomach drops for a second as the plane shudders, and I grip the armrests so hard that my knuckles turn white.

Max curses long and loud.

"It's fine," I say when the plane stabilizes. My heart is pounding in my chest and I swallow hard. "Turbulence is normal."

"That much?" Max asks, incredulous, eyes wide. "We dropped!"

"Only for a second," I say. I can feel myself calming down. Once, while flying over Germany, the plane I was on dropped nearly 200 feet. That had been way scarier.

There's a *ding* and the crackle of the P.A. system. "Ladies and gentleman," one of the pilots says, "I've turned the 'fasten seat belt' sign on. Please return your seatbacks and tray tables to their upright positions. We're expecting some turbulence and are going to see if we can get around it without too much trouble. Flight attendants, please return to your seats immediately."

"Okay," Max says, thumbing the seat button so she's sitting upright again. "That doesn't sound too bad."

Henry slips into the flight attendant seat next to his coworker and pulls the heavy straps over his shoulders. He struggles a minute to get his blue vest out of the way of the buckle but eventually manages. When he looks up, catching my eye, he attempts to smile reassuringly.

Is it just me or does that smile look a little strained?

The thought is chased from my head as the plane shudders, jostling everyone violently. The engines whine and we gain altitude for a brief moment before another round of rough air shakes the plane. An overhead bin snaps open, revealing a small, black backpack and a leopard print bag.

"Oh," Max says, seeing the bag. "That's mine! It's got my computer in it." She goes to unbuckle her seat belt.

I slap her hands away, stomach rolling with the plane. "What are you *doing*?"

"I need my bag," she tells me as she unsnaps her seat belt. "Come on, it'll just take a sec—"

She breaks off as the plane drops again, throwing

her up toward the ceiling. I scream when her head connects with a solid *thud*, and again when a shift to the right makes her hit the window. The plane levels out and she's thrown back into her seat like a rag doll.

"Max!" I twist in my seat, hands shaking as I push at her shoulder. "Max!"

She doesn't respond. The hit must have made her fall unconscious. I fumble for her seat belt, armrest digging into my stomach as I lean over, and yank it out from under her butt. I buckle it for her and pull it tight across her hips, snapping back into my seat just as another rough patch hits.

The P.A. crackles. "We are having a rough time getting out of this storm. Please remain seat—"

The lights die at the same time as the P.A., plunging the cabin into darkness. I become aware of people shouting and screaming and grit my teeth to keep from joining them. From behind me I hear Mr. Wilkins yelling my name. I really wish I hadn't changed seats now.

Next to me, Max groans. "Ow, wha . . . ?"

I can't answer her. I tuck my head between my knees, folding my hands over my neck and head. *It's just turbulence, it's just turbulence . . .*

Air masks drop from the ceiling as we fall again, the bright yellow a sudden shock under the emergency lighting. I snatch one out of the air and slam it over my face, over-tightening the straps until they cut into my skin. The cord stretches with me as I tuck back down. Out of the corner of my eye, I see Max, upright and wild-eyed, looking around the cabin.

The plane shudders and dives again, provoking more screams. I count in my head, waiting for the pilots to pull up.

One, two, three . . .

Pull back up. Dive again.

. . . four, five, six . . .

Pull back up. Dive again.

"BRACE YOURSELF," Henry bellows.

. . . seven, eight, nine . . .

The next time the plane tips down, it doesn't go back up.

CHAPTER 2

THE SOUND OF METAL TWISTING AND GRIND-
ing fills my head. I can't hear anyone screaming,
not even myself, over the terrible noise. It's hot, and
I'm terrified we'll burst into flames in midair. All I
can see is the blue of the seat because I'm hunched
over with my head between my legs. My fingernails
are cutting into the back of my neck and my heart
is pounding so fast that I can barely feel individual
beats anymore.

The plane bucks again, rattling and tearing in a
desperate fight to stay in the air. I'm being thrown
around in my seat with each jerk, seat belt digging

painfully into my hips. I feel like we've been dropping forever . . . and yet it seems like no time at all.

Then there's another great lurch. I hear windows shattering as the metal of the plane screams louder and louder. We hit the ground and the force of it makes my chest feel like it's breaking open over my knees. All the breath leaves my lungs and I desperately try to suck in air, but fail.

I black out.

- - -

I don't know how long I'm out. A minute? An hour? I don't try to move when I come to; I don't do anything. I just sit and try to force oxygen into my body.

I think for a moment that this is it. It's over. We crashed.

Here's what they don't tell you in the movies: it's not over when you hit the ground.

"Unbuckle and exit! Remove your seat belt and get out!"

The voice is familiar and a murky image of the male flight attendant surfaces. Is he talking? I can't understand what he's saying.

"Take off your seat belt! Exit the plane!" He sounds as winded as I feel and his words are slurring together.

We crashed, I think. *I need to move. I need to get out. I need to get out.*

I sit up slowly, using my hands to pull myself up. The other passengers are still slumped over in their seats. There's light, a lot of it, but I can't see the front half of the plane. It looks like it's been ripped off.

Shakily, my hands go to the belt at my waist. My fingers fumble along where the band is cutting into my hips and eventually hit the metal center clumsily. I can't figure out the buckle for an unnerving moment but manage to pull the latch almost by accident. The straps fall to either side of me.

Next step: get out of the plane.

The effort it takes to stand doesn't seem possible.

I can barely feel my legs and it's through willpower alone that I force my knees to straighten, my arms holding my upper body upright by grabbing onto the seat in front of me. I stand as straight as I'm able.

I step out into the aisle and my legs promptly go out from underneath me. I'm too shocked to register the fall. I'm on the floor before I know it and there's something sharp and cold underneath me.

I groan and try to get away from the debris stabbing me in the stomach by rolling over. My shoulder hits the metal of the seats, preventing me from lying on my back.

I need to get up. I need to get out of the plane. I brace myself for the pain of getting up.

There's a popping sound, or something that sounds like popping to my damaged ears. I watch the ceiling above me turn red and orange. I feel my shock break as if I'm doused in cold water.

The plane is on fire.

Get out.

I crawl free of the wreckage on my hands and

knees, coughing black smoke from my lungs. I can hear people crying and screaming.

"Please!" the male flight attendant shouts again. "Unbuckle your seat belts and exit the plane!"

His words make sense now and I turn, blinking under the bright sun. My breath catches and I cough for a long moment, eyes watering as I stare in horror. The plane is a mess of warped metal and dark soot, flames licking at the rear. The cockpit looks like it's detached completely and I see someone lying face-down next to it. They're not moving.

"Help! I need help," a woman calls from inside the only part of the cabin that's remained intact. Someone in a blue vest stumbles out of the hole in the side of the plane, tripping on debris. A man yells out and there's the sound of something heavy hitting glass. There's ringing in my ears and it's so hard to think.

The flight attendant—Hank? Hal? Henry?— comes to stand next to me, hands reflexively tugging on his blue vest. His brown hair is in disarray and strands are falling across his sweaty forehead and into his hazel eyes. I stare up at him. There's blood on his face.

"Gloria," he says, "right?"

My brow furrows. "Y-yes." My tongue feels thick and clumsy in my mouth and it takes effort to think. "My name is Gloria."

"I'm Henry," he says. "Do you remember me? I helped you find your new seat?"

My mind seems to be working a little faster and I nod slowly. He'd moved me away from Mr. Wilkins. *Mr. Wilkins.* "Yeah."

"Good, that's good," Henry says. "Listen, Gloria, I'm going to need your help, okay? Some people are stuck and I need your help to get them unstuck."

"I . . . they're still in the plane," I say. "There's fire." Something in my chest hurts when I think about going back in there and I think the panic shows on my face.

"You don't have to go in," Henry says. His eyes dart back to the wreck and he takes a deep breath.

"Just tell people to come to you, okay? Everyone is really confused right now and they need you to tell them what to do."

He doesn't wait for me to agree before reentering the wreck. I can see him ducking under flung-open luggage compartments, stepping over a seat that's been ripped free of the floor, and then stepping out of sight into the cabin.

I sway on the spot and swallow hard. The plane is small but it had been full at takeoff. I'd counted the seats as I went by and there were thirty people in there. My eyes stray to a man lying on the ground and I feel all the air whoosh out of me. There are less than thirty people in there now.

I'm moving before I realize what I'm doing, hopping over glittering glass and chunks of metal on the ground. I duck inside the plane and stay low, eyes still watering from the dark smoke that's rolling along the cabin's ceiling.

"Mr. Wilkins?" I call. I cough and squint into the aisle. There are people hanging into it or lying on the ground. From this low, I can't see much above the armrests. "Max?"

I inch forward, coming to the first row of seats. There's a woman by the window, not moving. I crawl over the armrest of the aisle seat, keeping my head down, and reach out to grab her shoulder. My fingers touch something wet but I ignore it, shaking her.

"Ma'am? Ma'am, we need to get out of the plane." I stop shaking her, an eerie feeling coming over me. She's not responding and she's not moving. My eyes trace over her weathered face, down her neck, and stop. There's red there—dark red—and something wet and meaty-looking. I jerk my hand away and look at the skin of my palm. It's red and sticky with her blood.

I recoil hard enough that I fall back into the aisle, flat on my butt. I know with an unwavering certainty that the woman is dead. I don't need to see her eyes or even look for her pulse. No one's neck looks like that while they're alive.

I force myself to keep going. There are more people on the plane and I have to find Mr. Wilkins. The next row of seats is empty but there's an old man lying in the aisle, cradling his arm to his chest. It jerks with his uneven breath and I swallow reflexively when I see it's very clearly broken.

"Hey," I say, dropping down. My hands flutter around his head and shoulders. "Can you move? You need to get out of the plane."

The man stares at me uncomprehendingly and I move my head to a better angle in case seeing my lips will help. "The plane isn't safe. Can you walk?"

He licks his lips, smearing blood onto them. I really hope it's from biting his cheek and not something worse. "Y-yes."

"Great," I say. My voice is way too high but I try to sound confident anyway. "Um, it's that way. Let me help you."

With my help, the man manages to get to his knees and turn around. When he tries to get me to go with him, I shake my head and point toward the exit. I watch him hobble outside, choking on the thick air, and then go to the next few seats.

I help a few people over some fallen luggage on their way out and rouse a couple more from their seats. I don't see Max and I pray that Henry got her out. I bet she was badly off after the turbulence tossed her around.

The air is getting a little better, the smoke clearing. Whatever was on fire must not be anymore, and I'm grateful. I cautiously move to a higher crouch that lets me get an idea of where I am in the plane. Though it feels like I've been creeping forward forever, I'm only about halfway to the back. I see Henry hunched over a prone form and doing chest compressions. I want to rush forward and see if it's Mr. Wilkins but I stop myself. Running could get me injured in the debris-strewn aisle and I need to help, not get hurt. I make myself go to the next seat, praying I don't find another dead person.

The image of the first woman flashes through my mind and I feel bile rising. I collapse against a seat, arms barely holding me upright as I fight not to vomit. It's so hot but cold chills are racing over my body and I know I have to get a grip. I have to find Mr. Wilkins. He'd know what to do.

"Mr. Wilkins?" I call. I reach out and use the next seat to pull me forward, stepping shakily over a briefcase. I catch sight of the top of his head, the salt-and-pepper hair unmistakable, and feel a surge of relief go through me. "Mr. Wilkins!"

I lunge forward, stumbling over a huge piece of what used to be an overhead bin, and stop cold. There are two people there, and the one that isn't Mr. Wilkins is hanging limply into the aisle.

The man's hair looks okay, not wet or dark with blood, and his hands are trailing along the floor. I reach out and gently lay a hand on him, heart sinking when he doesn't immediately move. I push at his shoulder until he rolls back toward the seat, revealing his chest and head.

This time I can't stop the bile, and I spin away toward the empty seats across the aisle to vomit.

My shoulders heave and I choke, eyes watering. His head . . . his head is cracked open like an egg, revealing thick, grey tissue and so much *blood*.

There's nothing to do for it. I have to get to Mr. Wilkins. I wipe my mouth with the back of my hand and turn back around. My eyes skitter over the wound and I try to ignore the way the dead man flops as I try to tug him out of his seat. It's like he's caught on something though, because no matter how much strength I use, he doesn't move at all.

"Let me help." Big hands come past me to grab the dead man's shirt collar and I jump in surprise. The boy from across the aisle—the cute one—lets go and holds his hands up. "I just want to help. He's your dad, right?" He points to Mr. Wilkins, who is unresponsive.

"This guy's stuck," I say instead of answering the question. Mr. Wilkins had been teaching me music since I was in fourth grade. He picked me up from school and made me snacks and helped me with my homework. He practically lived at my house when my parents went to perform, often coming up with ridiculous reasons for why he should stay, barely disguising the fact that he didn't want me to be alone. My heart is in my throat and I yank on the guy again, trying to dislodge him.

"Stop, stop," the boy says. He nudges me out of the way and I can see blood staining his jersey. "Let me check for a seat belt." He finds it after a moment and the metal click is loud. "On the count of three."

We heave the body out of the way. I nearly go down over a briefcase as I fall back under the man's weight. I bite off a scream as his head lands wetly on my shoulder. Panic rises but the boy pulls the body off me almost immediately. With a surprising amount of strength, he lays the body across a row of seats.

"Okay," he pants. "Do you need help getting your dad out?"

"Please," I say. I don't want to lift Mr. Wilkins up. What if his head flops over? What if his neck is torn up? What if the front of his head is caved in? I grit my teeth. "I'll unbuckle him."

It takes a bit of maneuvering but we manage to get Mr. Wilkins out into the aisle. He's a couple inches short of six feet, which makes it easier than it was with his much-larger seat partner. The boy takes most of Mr. Wilkins's weight, and when we get clear of the biggest stack of luggage, throws Mr. Wilkins's arm over his shoulder and takes him out of the plane by himself. My muscles are screaming at me for over-exerting them so I don't protest and just focus on keeping up.

We emerge out onto the hot ground and the boy lowers Mr. Wilkins. I collapse next to Mr. Wilkins, relieved to see that he doesn't seem to have any obvious injuries other than a small cut at his temple that's surrounded by a darkening bruise.

"He's alive," I say, voice breaking with relief. I reach out and shake his shoulder. "Mr. Wilkins? Mr. Wilkins!"

"He'll wake up eventually," the boy tells me.

He pushes his sweaty hair out of his face and looks around us. "Wow, we're lucky to be alive."

I know he must be seeing what I saw—the twisted frame of the plane and a pilot's body lying outside of the cockpit. I keep my eyes on Mr. Wilkins and say, "Thank you for helping me get him out."

"I saw you helping out my coach," the boy says. "The guy with the broken arm? Friedman's good people and I had to pay that back. I'm Travis." He holds his hand down to me to shake. It's covered in blood and dirt, just like mine.

I shake it and then let him pull me to my feet. "Gloria." I glance back at the plane, brow furrowing. "Do you think anyone else is in there? Maybe we should—"

"Everyone alive is out," Henry says, startling Travis and me. Henry's curly hair is black with smoke and his mouth is pressed into a grim line. "Is he injured? Let's get him over to Sylvia. She's got EMT training."

"Mr. Wilkins knows CPR," I say,

remembering his words from the plane. We all look at Mr. Wilkins, unconscious on the ground. "When . . . when he wakes up, he can help."

Henry softens a little. "You got it."

He and Travis pick Mr. Wilkins up. Everyone is gathered in one spot, some lying on bright yellow plastic that I recognize from the safety pamphlets as a raft. Others are staring in shock at the plane and then blinking into the distance as if trying to put two and two together. The other flight attendant is darting around the deflated raft, putting pressure on wounds and ordering people to start ripping cloth for bandages.

"Get the first aid kit," she says to Henry as we approach. "Why I didn't think—it's in the overhead with the blankets. There's another in the cockpit. We'll need both. Is that another one? Lay him here."

I think this must be Sylvia by the way Henry immediately obeys her, laying Mr. Wilkins down on the plastic next to Max. I'm gratified to see Max but am scared by the horrific-looking cut on her arm that extends up over her bicep and onto her shoulder. Whatever cut her completely shredded her shirt and flannel.

I squint beyond our little ragged group to see flat land, low shrubs, and not much else. A distance away I can see a ridgeline very faintly. Maybe some low hills. It's hot and my throat seizes when I look in the other direction and see the same thing.

"We crashed in the desert," Travis says from beside me. He sounds stunned. "*The desert.*"

I almost disagree with him. The desert is sandy and in Egypt, it's not *this*. This is dry and cracked and sparsely populated with sagebrush and Joshua trees. This looks a lot like where I live in California.

Which is the desert. My mouth shuts with a click. In the movies, they never crash in the desert. They always crash in water or in a jungle or something. Somewhere where there's more than a couple of tough plants and dirt.

"Gloria, Travis," Henry says, jerking me out of my horror. He gestures back toward the plane and then winces as it pulls his sore muscles. "Will you help me get supplies?"

Travis and I follow him. Above us, the storm clouds move to block the sun again.

CHAPTER 3

"That's the last of it," Henry tells us. He hands Travis another case of water and me another box of airline pretzels. Outside, we can still hear Sylvia barking orders, directing people where to put the injured. She'd made Henry inflate the emergency rafts so she could use them as makeshift stretchers, and then sent him and us back for more supplies.

Travis sets the water outside the plane and purses his lips. "People need to stay hydrated when it's this hot. Is this all the water?"

"Unfortunately," Henry says. He shades his eyes and looks up. The major storm clouds are almost gone and it's insanely hot each time the sun peeks through.

"When do you think rescue will come save us?" Travis asks, frowning at the small stack of water. There are bottles from the flight attendant area and a dozen or so from passenger carry-ons. "This won't last us long unless we ration it."

"It shouldn't take that long for them to show up," I say. "I mean, an entire plane can't just disappear."

"No, it can't," Travis says, perking up. "They have flight plans and stuff to track us with!"

"We deviated from our flight plan. We're not on it anymore," Henry says. At our horrified expressions, he hastens to add, "But every flight has a black box. It records our flight and also sends out a sort of homing beacon they can follow."

"Good," I say, thinking of the lack of signal on my phone. It had been worth a shot. "I don't think there's a cell tower around here."

Henry's eyes get a faraway look. "But the beacon doesn't reach very far," he says quietly.

Travis makes a frustrated sound. "There might not even be a town around here. If we are in Arizona—"

"We are," Henry assures us, snapping back to focus.

"—then it could be thirty miles to civilization." Travis pauses, his face pinched into a look of fear. "Or more."

"We're supposed to stay with the plane anyway," Henry says, trying to be comforting. "That way they can find us."

I nod. "I'm going to go check on Mr. Wilkins." I turn my back on the wreckage and head over to where the other passengers have gathered.

I can't help the way my eyes dart all around on the way over. Miles and miles of desert stretch out to the horizon. Those hills I saw earlier look even farther away now, and the sky yawns above us ominously. We're so exposed and I feel really, really vulnerable. I shudder. Hopefully rescue will show up sooner rather than later.

The first thing Sylvia did with the supplies she asked for was lay out all the airplane blankets so that the wounded weren't lying on the dirt. The rafts she'd used to move people are now piled up, the bright yellow stained with blood and soot. There are a couple of people with what appear to be sprains and bruises sitting on one section of blanket, staring numbly out into the distance. The severely wounded—five all told including Mr. Wilkins—are lying supine on top of another section of blankets. Sylvia is hunched down next to them, and the remaining passengers, all adults, are standing in a circle and talking. I go to edge between them and the sitting group to make my way over to Mr. Wilkins.

"Oh no, oh no, oh no no no," one woman is repeating over and over again. She's sitting with her back to everyone else, facing me, and I can see that her eyes are wide and unseeing. She's rocking back and forth. I stop about ten feet from everyone, a little freaked out.

"Shut up!" says a man from the standing group.

His red hair is thinning at the top of his head and the business suit he's wearing is torn and covered in soot. He turns away from the others and glares down at the rocking woman. "Some of us are trying to think!"

The woman doesn't seem to hear him. "No, no, no, no . . . "

Enraged, the red-haired man takes an aggressive step forward, blocking my path in between the two groups. He's big, with a mean set to his jaw. His hands clench and unclench. "Shut up!"

"Hemming!" a woman snaps from behind him. She's dressed in a pantsuit and has thin, ragged hair. She folds her arms over her chest. "Leave it."

Hemming ignores her. He squats abruptly and grabs the rocking woman roughly by the arm. "Stop!" He shakes her so hard that her head snaps back and forth. It reminds me of the dead people I'd seen in the plane and my stomach turns over.

"Hey!" The older man I'd helped—Coach Friedman—storms over from where he'd been getting treatment from Sylvia. He's limping heavily and his arm is in a sling but he still gets right into Hemming's space. "Leave her alone!"

Hemming lurches to his feet, his face going blotchy and red. "She's driving me insane!"

"Then take a walk," Coach Friedman suggests. His eyes are hard and he jerks his chin to a random expanse of desert. "Cool your head."

Hemming stares at Coach Friedman, chest heaving. Then, without a word, he spins on his heel and marches off. I can see him pull out his cell phone on the way, furiously trying to get a signal.

The woman in the pantsuit looks at Coach Friedman appraisingly. Coach Friedman ignores her, instead dropping down to the rocking woman's side. He begins talking to her in a low voice and, after a minute, her rocking gradually peters out.

I take the opportunity to slide past them all, trying not to be noticed. Hemming may have taken a walk but the others in the standing group look like they're pretty upset. I make it to where Mr. Wilkins is and I release a breath I didn't know I'd been holding. I drop down next to him and frown at how pale he is. Why hasn't he woken up?

"He's coming around," Sylvia tells me without looking up. She's carefully lifting a stained shirt from the stomach of one of the injured and peering underneath. "What's our food and water situation like?"

I tell her about the small stack of water bottles and smaller stack of pretzels and snacks while I watch Mr. Wilkins. His eyelids are fluttering every so often, dragging up with effort before flicking down. His fingers twitch against the blankets and he groans.

"Mr. Wilkins!" I gently help him to a sitting position, wincing each time he exhales in pain. "Are you okay? What hurts?"

"Water," Mr. Wilkins croaks. He grimaces, licking his lips. "Please."

I practically fly back to the plane, rip a bottle out of the case, ignore Travis and Henry's surprised exclamations, and sprint back to the shelter. I'm sweating a lot when I skid onto my knees and crawl the rest of the way to Mr. Wilkins's side. I wrench open the bottle and hold it to his lips with difficulty since my hands are shaking. He takes a few sips and then raises a hand as if to take it from me. Sylvia's hand stops him.

"Not quite yet," she says to Mr. Wilkins, her sharp, hawkish features tight. She gently takes the bottle and recaps it, taking his wrist in her other hand. "Pulse is weak and your pupils aren't equal. You probably hit your head."

Mr. Wilkins frowns down at where her nails bite into the sensitive skin under his arm. "I—I don't remember." He looks at the capped bottle in her other hand. "Please. Water."

"Only a little more," Sylvia says. She twists off the cap and helps Mr. Wilkins take a few more swallows. She eases him back to the ground and starts over to another injured passenger, taking the water with her. "Don't tire him out. He needs to rest."

Mr. Wilkins's hand rises weakly and he sets it on

my knee. I realize he's trying to pat it comfortingly, like he did on the plane. "Are you okay?"

A lump rises in my throat. "I'm okay." I want to tell him about what I've been doing but I don't think telling him about the dead is a good idea. "We're waiting to be rescued."

"Ah," Mr. Wilkins says and grimaces.

"It should be soon!" My chest feels tight. I hope I'm telling the truth. "Henry—the flight attendant—thinks they'll track the plane." *But what if they aren't close enough to pick up the beacon?* I keep the doubt to myself.

"No, no, not 'ah,'" Mr. Wilkins says. His grimace transforms into what he intended from the start—a smile. "Awesome."

I laugh until I start crying.

CHAPTER 4

RESCUE DOESN'T COME AN HOUR LATER OR two hours later or even three hours later. All of us that can are scanning the cloudy skies, trying to make out any speck or line that could be another plane or a helicopter.

Sylvia goes around handing out water bottles, telling everyone to stay hydrated and not to move too much or else they'll lose too much water. Henry helps, checking in with the passengers who've just woken and speaking quietly with Coach Friedman and Travis.

I stay by Mr. Wilkins's side. Every minute that

passes without rescue causes the ball of dread in my stomach to grow and grow. I wrap my arms around my knees, ignoring the blood that's soaked into my clothes and the dirt that covers the rest of me.

Around us, night falls. And as night falls, so does the temperature.

"Oh, man," Max groans from next to me. She woke an hour after Mr. Wilkins. While she doesn't have a concussion, the cut on her shoulder is bad enough that she can't wrap the blanket as tightly around herself as she'd like. "Why didn't we build a fire?"

I don't answer her, teeth chattering. It's so cold that even pressed against both Max and Mr. Wilkins, I can't sleep. I see that the other passengers are in a similar boat. I can hear several people crying and I cover my ears, trying to block them out.

We thought rescue would be here by now, I think in response to Max. *That's why*. Why build a fire when we'd be flying out of here before nightfall? We didn't know. And now all we can do is shiver and ride it out until morning, listening desperately for the sound of help arriving.

\- \- \-

I manage to fall asleep, though I don't know how. When I wake up, I blink at the blue sky and assess my position. I'm still curled up with Max and Mr. Wilkins, their body heat barely working its way through my blankets, and my entire body hurts. The cold has made my joints stiff and I groan as I sit upright, blinking sleep from my eyes.

My skin prickles as I see the endless expanse of desert all around us. There are people lying curled up all around me, apparently no one brave enough to spend the night in the plane, and there's no smoke coming from the wreck.

Rescue never came.

Everyone begins to show signs of waking up, groaning and stretching. One by one they all have the same realization. The crying people from last night are dead-eyed now, unable to expend the energy to continue weeping. Hemming curses the sky and storms away, pulling out his cell phone again.

"They're coming," Mr. Wilkins says. I jump at his voice and he smiles weakly at me. "Don't worry, they're coming." He offers me a bottle of water.

I sip the water slowly and watch everyone. Some people aren't waking up, even though the sun is climbing in the sky. I watch Sylvia kneel next to one of the injured and shake his shoulder. She shakes him harder, and when he doesn't respond, she places two fingers at his neck. After a long moment, she shakes her head and moves on to the next still figure.

"Why—what's wrong with them?" Max asks her, unnerved, like me, to see the action.

Sylvia, dropping next to another wounded person a few feet from us, shakes her head. "Exposure. Their cores got too cold because of their injuries. They're dead." She pulls a blanket over the patient in front of her and moves on to the next.

"Mr. Wilkins was a wedding violinist," I blurt out to Max. I'm trying to make a distraction so we don't stare at the number of covered people all around us. "Tell her about the weird wedding!"

Mr. Wilkins shakes himself and tears his eyes away from the dead. "Hmmm? Oh, yes, well, not every musician can be in the Philharmonic. For a number of years I played weddings—"

I let the cadence of the familiar story comfort me, gratified to see that Max is just as interested as I was to know why the bride had a goat walk her down the aisle. I close my eyes and focus on Mr. Wilkins's voice. I'll never tell him but I'm glad that his wedding gig days are over. I'd probably have given up the violin a long time ago if it weren't for him.

Eventually Mr. Wilkins's voice starts fading as his eyelids droop. He turns down the food and water I offer him, insisting that he needs to rest. He covers himself completely with a blanket to protect his skin from the sun, and goes to sleep.

I stare out at the sky, peripherally aware of Max

following Mr. Wilkins's lead and going to sleep. It's getting hotter and I can feel my body wanting to sleep too but I don't let it. I have to keep watch in case rescue comes.

It's only about a half hour into my vigil when Travis calls me over to the plane for a meeting. The passengers who are capable of standing are already over there, clustered in a tight group and speaking in low, worried tones. They've been at it since Sylvia covered the last person.

The group is comprised mostly of adults, with Travis standing with his arms crossed over his chest on the outskirts. I move to stand next to him silently, not wanting to interrupt.

"—aren't close to *something*," Coach Friedman is saying. His broken arm is in a clean, makeshift sling and his stern, blue eyes are bright. "You could be walking for days!"

"It's not the Sahara," Hemming snarks back. He's got deep bags under his eyes and he looks just as angry as he did yesterday. "We're bound to hit *something*. And it's better than waiting out here doing *nothing*."

"Listen," Henry says, holding his hands out pleadingly. "I know it seems bad but rescue *is* coming. All we have to do is wait—"

"And what if it isn't?" the rocking woman asks. Her eyes flit over the group and she pulls at her torn blouse. "Maybe they missed us. Maybe we're going to be out here for *weeks*. What do we do then? What if—"

"Alexis," Sylvia interrupts, laying a hand on the woman's arm. "You're not helping." She looks at the others, expression tight. "We should start rationing. Just in case."

"We can't survive on tiny pretzels," the woman in the pantsuit says. She tries to run a hand through her thin, blond hair but has to give up the effort as the tangles prove too tough to comb through. "Hemming's right. We have the water now, we should take our chances and see if we can find a town."

Coach Friedman thrusts his chin out. "And the people who can't walk? What about you?" He turns to a thin-faced man who's been nodding along to what the woman and Hemming have been saying. "You really think you can make it on that knee?"

"Um," the thin-faced man says. His beady eyes dart from the coach to Hemming and back. "I—"

"He can if he wants to live," Hemming announces. "We all will."

"Whoa," Henry says holding his hands up, "this isn't life and death yet. We were scheduled to land in Burbank. They'll come for us, trust me."

Sylvia snorts. "That's if we weren't kicked too far out of the way." She rubs the back of her neck. "We've got some seriously injured people. Three of them died last night and I know a couple more won't last through this night."

My blood runs cold and I step forward without thinking. "What? Who?" I push past the business people with too much force. "What is that supposed to mean?"

"Gloria," Henry says, putting himself in between Sylvia and me. "This isn't the time."

I see red. "She just said they won't make it through the night! And these jerks just want to save themselves! What is wrong with you people?" *What about Mr. Wilkins?*

"Nothing," Hemming says. He squares his shoulders and sneers down at me. "It's the most logical course of action. Those of us who can will go find a town or village or whatever and then we'll—" he flaps a hand dismissively "—send someone here for the injured."

"It's smarter to stay put and conserve resources," Coach Friedman asserts, talking over my head. "A group of people on the move will need a lot more water than a group saving their strength!"

He's got a point but I can't let go of what Sylvia said. What did she mean that the injured won't last the night? "What if they don't get here in time? What if you don't find a town?" I can feel myself getting even angrier and I scowl at Hemming. "Your plan is stupid!"

Hemming's jaw clenches. "The grown-ups are talking, little girl."

My mouth drops open. Really? Little girl? "I'm *fourteen*," I say.

"Yeah," Hemming says condescendingly. "So why do we have to stand here and be judged by *you*?" He's forced to step back as Henry pulls me behind him.

"That little girl," Henry says in a low voice, "was one of the only ones to go back into the wreck to help the rest. She got out the supplies we do have. What did you do again, Hemming?"

"He walked around trying to find a cell signal for two hours," Travis says. He pushes through the group until he's standing next to me. Although he's about my age, he's a bit bigger than most of the adults. "Next time you talk to her like that, you and I are going to have a problem." I see Coach

Friedman nod approvingly out of the corner of my eye.

"Now's not the time to fight," the woman in the pantsuit says. She once again tries to run a hand through her thin hair and the wrinkles on her forehead deepen when she, once again, can't. Frustrated, she throws her arms in the air. "We have to come up with *some* sort of plan before the sun goes down. I am *not* spending another night like last night."

"Sarah's right," the thin-faced man says. His nervous fidgeting contradicts his confident tone. He pulls at his ruined suit and won't meet Coach Friedman's eyes.

Coach Friedman pinches the bridge of his nose. "It's going to get cold tonight. We know that now. We should focus on making a shelter today. And a fire."

"How long do you think we're going to be here?" Alexis asks. She hugs herself and begins rocking again. "Another day? Two? I have kids, I can't be stranded out here!"

"Calm down," Henry says authoritatively. "Look, we need to stay with the plane. Rescue will probably be here soon—"

"—but until then we need to focus on shelter," Coach Friedman interrupts definitively. "What are we going to do for warmth tonight?"

The conversation moves to figuring out how to make a fire. I don't know anything about it so I find myself pushed to the edges of the group, Travis still tense next to me. I glance at him from the corner of my eye. He looks just as tired as I feel but he'd still stepped up for me.

"Thanks," I say. I pull my hoodie's sleeve over my hand and use it to wipe at my face. "For sticking up for me."

"That guy was being a jerk," Travis says quietly. He watches the group of adults for another moment and sighs irritably. "Come on. If they want to make a fire and build a shelter, we need to clear some brush away."

"Yeah, okay. We shouldn't move the injured

though, not until it's ready. Maybe over there?" I point to a relatively flat part of the desert, about twenty feet from where Mr. Wilkins, Max, and the other injured people are sleeping.

Travis nods and leads the way to the area I indicated. It's a good distance away from the plane so Travis says we probably don't have to worry about jet fuel or anything. He starts yanking up the small, hardy desert plants and, after a moment, I follow suit.

Max sits up, blanket pooling around her waist, and asks, "What are you guys doing?" She stands up slowly and shuffles close to us. Her curly hair is flat on one side and she has taken off her flannel, probably judging it unsalvageable.

"Making a place for a shelter," I tell her. The sage is rough on my hands and I find it's easier to reach down to the base and pull it up by the roots. "You okay?"

"Couple of busted ribs. The cut is all show, or so Sylvia says," says Max as she sits down with a groan.

Her upper body is wrapped in grey fabric that's stained dark with drying blood. She leans over with a pained grunt and wraps a hand around the base of a small plant. She gives it an experimental tug and scowls when it doesn't do anything. "What were you guys talking about over there?" She watches appreciatively as Travis pulls up a sizeable plant. "And who are you?"

I let Travis introduce himself and recap what had happened. I thought I'd missed out on most of the conversation but, apparently, it had just been what I heard—the adults arguing about whether they'd stay by the plane or try to find a town.

The sun is climbing quickly, bringing heat with it. It doesn't take long for sweat to start dripping from my hairline and into my eyes as I work. I think that's why I don't see the snake before I am *way* too close.

The rattle is loud, especially from three feet away. Both Travis and Max stop talking, freezing in place.

"Is that," Travis asks, "a rattlesnake?" He takes a

careful step closer and then stops, eyes scanning the ground for the thing, just like me.

I finally see the snake and I feel my hands go numb with fear. Yep, that's a snake. A three-foot-long, *huge*, venomous snake. I lift my foot and slowly take a step back, wincing as it draws its diamond shaped head back, ready to strike. My next step back is a little faster and the one after that even faster.

I end up running into Travis, who's forced to wrap his arms around me to keep us both from falling. I stumble but eventually catch my balance with his help, eyes never leaving the rattlesnake. After a long, heart-stopping moment, it stops rattling and, very slowly, begins to slither away.

It occurs to me that there isn't any anti-venom out here. If I'd gotten bit I might have died. I might have *died*. I say, "Oh my God."

"What if there are more?" Max demands. In her fear, she's managed to gain her feet and is pale and sweating. "Oh my God, what else wants to kill us in the desert?"

"Scorpions," I say without thinking. I wince. "Maybe? Maybe there aren't any around here."

"No, there are," Travis says grimly. He flips over a rock and points. "Little ones, probably not too venomous."

"Probably," Max echoes. "*Probably.*"

Travis's lips press into a thin line and he picks up the rock. He tosses it after the snake and sighs. "Not much we can do but watch out for them."

"I'll be over *there*," Max says. She jerks a thumb toward the other side of the blankets, farthest away from where the snake disappeared. "Away from all of *that.*" She casts a disgusted look at where the snake had gone and starts making her way to Mr. Wilkins.

Shaking my head, I get back to work. We clear an area for the shelter without much trouble, though both Travis and I are careful to shake each plant to scare off any nasty critters. Max brings us some of the blankets not in use and we lay them out on the newly cleared space.

"We need shade," Travis says, frowning at the

blanket floor. He wipes sweat from his face with the back of his hand. He looks around and spots some of the suitcases that the others had managed to get from the wreck. "We could use those as supports?"

I spot the rafts Sylvia had used to move the injured. The blood on them has dried into gross brown spots but they're whole and big. "We can use those as the roof."

Travis grins and claps me on the back. "Good idea." He has dimples underneath the dirt.

I duck my head so he can't see me blush and hurry over to start dragging the rafts to our cleared spot. Travis starts emptying suitcases and stacking them as supports.

"Oooh," Max says, arching an eyebrow and grinning. "Gloria and Travis, sitting in a tree—"

"Shut up," I mutter, face burning. I pull one of the rafts toward me and am surprised by its lightness. It's not too heavy, thankfully, and I'm able to drag it away without too much difficulty.

"Oh, Travis," Max says in a high-pitched voice. "I have a *lot* of good ideas—ow!"

"Sorry," I say innocently, moving the raft so it's not bumping her anymore. "I slipped."

Max scowls at me, rubbing her shoulder.

By the time I get both rafts over to the cleared space, Travis has six stacks of suitcases, all coming up to about four feet high. They're spaced so that the rafts will sit side by side on top of them. Travis leans down, picks up one of the rafts by himself, wobbles a little under its bulk, and then sets it down perfectly on top of four of the stacks with only a small grunt of effort.

"You're really strong," I say, impressed. I ignore Max's giggles from behind me and will my face to remain blush-free. "Do you play sports?"

"Yeah," Travis says, wiping his face with the hem of his jersey before holding it out for me to read. "Football."

"You any good?" I ask. It's the same question he'd

asked me on the plane before it crashed and, judging by his smile, he remembers.

"Very good," he says, "not to brag or anything. That's actually why I was flying to California. A college scouted me and invited me for a tour." He lifts the second raft and, with my guidance, gently sets it down so it's on the two remaining stacks of luggage and the edge of the first raft.

"Wow," I say. That sounded like he was *really* good. "How old are you?"

"Seventeen," Travis says. He shrugs. "I'm graduating early. My parents enrolled me in a lot of summer school." His mouth twists. "A *lot* of summer school." He ducks down and crawls under our shelter, sitting in the shade. He pats the blanket next to him in invitation.

"I get sent to violin camp every year," I tell him. "I know how that feels." One of the stacks of luggage blocks my view of Max and her view of Travis and me. I feel myself relax a little.

"So were you just in a bad mood on the plane or

are you really not good at violin?" Travis asks. He leans back on his forearms. "If you don't mind me asking."

"Sorry about that," I say, abruptly feeling ashamed about the way I'd talked to him before. "I, um, actually just lost a pretty big competition so . . . " I shrug, trying to play it off.

"I know how *that* is," Travis says understandingly. "I can't tell you how many plays I've completely blown. Cost my high school team the championship in my freshman year." He shakes his head. "They never let me live that down." He sounds weirdly fond of the memory.

My brow furrows. "Isn't that . . . bad?"

Travis nods cheerfully. "*Super* bad. I nearly quit the team that year."

"Why didn't you?"

"Because I love playing football," Travis says. He grins and looks so open and relaxed that I can't help but grin back. "It took time for me to get good, sure, but what I really loved was being on the field, not being good. Don't you love violin?"

My grin dims and I look away. I don't know how to answer that. I used to like playing a lot but the last couple of years have been rough. Finally I say, "I don't know."

"Oh," Travis says, sounding taken aback. There's an awkward silence. "Then why do you keep playing?"

"I don't know," I say again. I wrap my arms around my knees. "I mean, I guess I don't hate it. I just . . . can't seem to get the notes right." I shake my head. "Enough about me. So you're on your high school's football team? Coach Friedman's your coach, right?"

Travis lets me change the subject. "Actually he's the baseball coach. He's just chaperoning me since my coach is busy. He's a cool guy." He starts crawling out from under the shelter. "We should start moving people in before they get too burned."

I follow him and help Max get under the new

shelter. Mr. Wilkins wakes up enough to let us help him too but some of the others we have to drag on blankets. Finally, we get everyone underneath it and out of the sun, settling in beside them.

We drink the last of the water that had been on the blankets and sit back to wait for the others. I can see them over by the plane still but don't pay attention past that. The heat is making me really tired and I find myself dozing off next to Travis.

Travis's groan wakes me a while later. The sun is still high in the sky but on its way down. I'd guess that it's about two or three o'clock. Travis rolls over, groaning again. "I would kill for some water right now."

"Wouldn't we all," I say. By my side, Max murmurs agreement. "I think Sylvia mentioned rationing though. We should probably ask her first."

Travis squints over at the plane, about a hundred feet away. "They're arguing again. I don't think now is a good time."

This isn't the time to argue and I'm surprised by

how angry it makes me. Adults always think they know best when they aren't even focusing on the right things.

"'To achieve great things, two things are needed: a plan, and not quite enough time,'" I say and stand up, brushing off my butt.

Travis turns and stares at me. "What?"

"It's what Mr. Wilkins tells me when I start practicing for a recital," I explain. My eyes flicker to my teacher's prone form and my heart stings. "It's a quote from Leonard Bernstein."

"I'll pretend to know who that is if you will," Max says to Travis, voice slurred from sleep.

I edge out from under the shelter and start walking toward the adults. "I'll be right back."

"Gloria!"

I don't stop, instead marching right up to the eight people who are *wasting time.* "Hey!"

Hemming's face sours as he catches sight of me. "We're talking."

"While you guys have been *talking,*" I say, "we've

actually been *doing* something. It's going to get cold tonight and we need a fire. We dug out an area for it but need, you know, the fire part. Do you guys know how to do that yet?"

"There are other more important considerations to be taken into account at this moment," Sarah says, folding her arms so her red nails rest delicately by the elbows of her crumpled pantsuit. "A long-term strategy for example."

"Uh huh," I say. I'm really not impressed by her professional tone. "And what about tonight? Right now? We built the shelter, if you didn't notice, but we need other stuff. The sun will go down and it's going to be dark and cold and we've already seen one rattlesnake. Have we decided how we're going to split up the water? The food? Should someone stay awake to watch for rescue or should we just hope for the best? What if it rains? What about—"

A big hand on my shoulder cuts me off and I look up to see Coach Friedman. "They get the point, I think." He regards the others evenly.

"She's right, we need to find a way to light this fire. Does anyone have any matches? A lighter?"

"I do," the thin-faced man says as everyone else shakes their heads. He looks at the wreck and pales, fidgeting. "It's, um, in my briefcase."

Coach Friedman nods. "We need to go through the cabin anyway, see if there's anything we can use in there."

"I'm not going," Sarah says immediately, lifting her chin. Three of the passengers murmur agreement, casting nervous glances at the dark opening into the main cabin.

"I'll go," I say and start just walking right over there, almost making Coach Friedman fall over on account of the grip he still has on my shoulder.

"Stuff needs to get done and if you all won't do it then I will." I turn and point at the thin-faced man. "What does your briefcase look like?" I ride the anger so I don't have to think about all the dead I'm about to see. My mouth is very, very dry.

"Brown with gold hardware," he says. I duck

into the cabin, ignoring everyone else. It's so simple that I don't see how they don't get it. The sun is going down. It will get cold. We need fire. We need a lighter. The lighter is in the plane.

I didn't really account for the dead though.

The inside of the plane smells like something bloated and rotten. It's hot—so much hotter than outside, which makes sense since the plane is basically a metal tube. The woman with her throat torn out looks different now and I feel my breath stop in my lungs at the sight of her. Her face is swollen, grotesquely drained of color, and her eyes are foggy. The blood on her neck is dark and sticky, and there are some small bugs that have begun to gather on the window by her head.

I force myself to look away and continue on, hands shaking. There's something viscerally horrifying about the sight and smell of the dead. It's like your hindbrain is telling you *danger* and *get away* all at once. I press on.

The briefcase the thin-faced man described is

exactly the one I was thinking of, the one in the aisle that I kept tripping over before. I snatch it from the floor and clutch it close to my chest, breathing hard.

I turn and run out of the cabin, stumbling over the turned-over drink cart at the entrance. Big hands catch me and steady me before lowering me to a sitting position. I curl up around the briefcase and try to get air into my lungs.

"Gloria, it's alright, just breathe."

"In and out, in and out."

"Is she okay?"

A plastic object is pressed against my arm and someone says, "Come on, let go. Here, take this. It's water."

I let them take the case from me and fumble for the bottle blindly. The woman's clouded eyes pop into my mind and I suck in a breath just as the water touches my lips. I cough, hard, and gag. *Get it together*. I take a slow, deep breath through my nose like I do before I perform. Then I exhale equally slowly. My eyes are closed and I enjoy the darkness, trying to banish the images of inside the cabin from my mind.

CHAPTER 5

EVENTUALLY I CALM DOWN ENOUGH THAT I can take a sip of water. It's warm but the liquid is like an electric shock to my system after what feels like days without it. I take a big gulp, not thinking of conserving *anything* at that point, and then another. When the bottle is half gone, I finally open my eyes to find Henry and Coach Friedman crouched in front of me with worried looks on their faces.

My cheeks color as I realize that I've just had a panic attack right in front of them, right after trying to be so cool about going into the plane. I look down at the bottle in my hands and twist it around, picking at the label before setting it down. "Um, thanks. Sorry."

"Don't be," Coach Friedman says. He sits back on his heels with a sigh, careful of his broken arm. "We shouldn't have let you go in alone. You did good, kid."

"You did," Henry agrees. He throws a quick look at Coach Friedman. "She's a force of nature, I swear."

"We need a couple of those around here," Coach Friedman says. "Come on, let's go rendezvous with the idiots."

I look around and finally notice that no one is by the plane with us. Instead, they're all grouped in front of the shelter Travis and I set up. There's a circle of rocks in front of it that hadn't been there before, inside of which is a pile of dry brush. Hemming and Travis are inside the circle and I can see a flicker of light every now and then as they attempt to get the sticks to catch.

I shove down everything as best I can, not

wanting to fall apart again in front of everyone. I take Coach Friedman's hand and let Henry grab my elbow, taking some of my weight so that the injured man doesn't have to. I follow Coach Friedman back to the shelter, still feeling the eyes from the plane. I rub my arms to ward off the goosebumps I feel coming.

"Don't forget this," Henry says, pressing the water bottle back into my hand. He shakes his head. "Sylvia's rationed it so we all only get six bottles each and Hemming is counting it as one of yours."

"Of course he is," I mutter under my breath, thinking of the mean-faced man. We're close enough that the others can hear us and I feel too shaken up to fight with Hemming right now. I skirt the edge of the group and make my way to Mr. Wilkins's side under the shelter.

The old woman with the white hair is sitting up, looking characteristically displeased. When she sees me, her eyebrows go way up. "You look like you've seen a ghost."

I ignore her and take Mr. Wilkins's hand between both of mine. He doesn't stir and I frown at how cold his skin is. I start rubbing my hands roughly over his, hoping the friction will warm him up.

The old lady—though she probably isn't yet into her sixties—doesn't seem to be put off by my silence. "I'm Mrs. Bloomingfield, dear. I suppose we ought to introduce ourselves since we seem to be stuck here for a while. I never imagined that the desert could be quite so hot. When I was your age, I lived in Michigan, you see, and we didn't need to worry about hot there, oh no. We had to worry about winter!"

I wish that she'd stop talking. It's sort of distracting me from trying to get Mr. Wilkins to wake up. I poke his cheek, right where he's getting a jowl wrinkle.

"Mr. Wilkins," I say, shaking his shoulder. "Mr. Wilkins." I think about the way Sylvia had shaken the dead people this morning. They hadn't stirred either. "Mr. Wilkins!"

Mr. Wilkins's eyes flutter open and he squints up at me. "Gloria? What's the matter?" His words slur into one another and I swallow down a fresh wave of worry.

"They're starting a fire," I say. "I think you should go sit by it to get warm."

"Don't worry about me," Mr. Wilkins says, only it sounds more like "Don' war buh meh." I can't tell if it's because he's just waking up or because of something worse.

"Your charge is very rude," Mrs. Bloomingfield says, nose in the air. "When I was a little girl—"

"Come on," I say to Mr. Wilkins. I haul his arm up and over my shoulders like I'd seen Travis do. "I think they've just about got it started."

It's awkward getting out of the shelter with Mr. Wilkins and not just because of the verbal lashing Mrs. Bloomingfield seems intent on giving me the entire time. The roof is low—about four feet off the ground—which means that I have to walk sort of hunched over. And Mr. Wilkins isn't very good at walking so I have to drag his entire bulk almost by myself. My muscles scream in protest each time he stumbles and drops more weight than he intends onto my shoulders. But eventually we make it, him groaning and me apologizing, over to the edge of the fire pit.

Travis and Coach Friedman are standing in identical, crossed-arm poses, shaking their heads, as Hemming crouches on the ground, blowing on a mass of loose, dry sagebrush. Sarah and her little following of businesspeople are off to the side, talking in hushed voices, with Sylvia the flight attendant putting in her two cents every once in a while. Alexis—the rocking woman—is fluttering at the fringes of their group. Henry is helping Max shrug into a big jacket that's from one of the suitcases, which is being used as an impromptu bench.

The sun has almost fully set by this point, only a thin glow showing where it has gone down. Stars have already started appearing in the rose-colored sky and the moon is half full and brighter than I've ever seen it. I think it might be beautiful but I don't really appreciate it because, in the light of the fire they've finally started, Mr. Wilkins doesn't look good. He doesn't look good at all.

I see that someone's brought over the stack of water bottles and snacks so I go over there to grab Mr. Wilkins a bottle. Just as I'm reaching for one, however, Hemming grabs my wrist.

"That'll be your second bottle tonight," Hemming says, eyes glittering. "You might want to ration better."

"It's not for me," I say acidly. I jerk my wrist out of his grip and wince as his nails scratch my skin. "*Ow*. It's for Mr. Wilkins."

Hemming sneers, eyes sliding to where Mr. Wilkins is listing to one side without me to support him. "Him? No, he doesn't get any."

I jerk, shocked. "Why not?"

"He's dying," Hemming says. He draws himself up to his full height, about a foot taller than me. "If we divide his share of the water amongst us, those who *actually* have a chance can last longer."

I can't believe what I'm hearing. My hands curl into fists. "He's fine. He just needs water." I don't recognize my own voice. It's cold and hard, not anything like the soft tones my parents prefer.

"What's going on here?" Henry asks cautiously, sidling up to us. We both ignore him.

"He is not fine," Hemming says, thrusting his chin out. "He'll be dead by morning."

My parents have always been fans of the phrase "turn the other cheek." They'd taught the phrase to me all through my childhood, insisting that it's better to take the higher road in a fight.

So it's really a toss-up over who's more surprised when I lunge for Hemming—me or him.

His surprise keeps him from acting long enough that my fist hits him right in the throat. He stumbles backwards, gurgling, and my eyes lock on his exposed stomach. My foot strikes out but, before it connects, a strong arm wraps around my stomach, reeling me backwards.

"Hey!" Henry shouts in my ear. "Quit it!"

This jerk doesn't know anything, I want to say but all that comes out of my mouth is an inarticulate scream of rage.

"You—you—," Hemming says. I don't know what he's trying to say but I know it probably isn't nice. That's fine, I'm not feeling very nice either.

"Take it back," I demand, struggling in Henry's arms. "You take it back!"

"What happened?" Coach Friedman asks, stalking up. He looks between Hemming and me, sees that Hemming isn't quite up to talking, and turns his bushy eyebrows toward me. "Gloria?"

I hit Henry's arms until he lets me down. "He said that Mr. Wilkins doesn't get any water because he'll—he'll be gone by morning." Heat rises up behind my eyes and I grit my teeth against the tears. I can't bring myself to say the word *dead*.

"It's a waste," Sarah says. She's gone up to

Hemming and has her arms wrapped around his shoulders as he massages his throat and glares at me wrathfully. "Hemming is right, if we ration without including the injured we'll have a chance."

"I agree," Mrs. Bloomingfield says. She's managed to get out of the shelter, following the scent of drama. Her leg wound doesn't seem to be hindering her at all now.

"You were one of the seriously injured this afternoon," Sylvia says with folded arms, as she and some of the others approach. "What, you got super healing?"

Mrs. Bloomingfield makes a face.

"Be that as it may," Coach Friedman says finally, "we can't take our chances with human life. What if one of them can recover but doesn't get the chance because we withheld food and water?"

Sylvia shakes her head. "I'm fairly confident in my assessment. Some of them need more help than we can give them. They need a doctor."

"There," Hemming says triumphantly. "They

need a doctor. There isn't one out here. Where does that leave us?"

"So we let them starve to death?" Travis asks, expression thunderous. "Die of thirst?"

Coach Friedman hesitates, expression conflicted.

"Oh, come on," I exclaim. I look around to see that many of the adults are shamefaced and won't meet my eyes. "They're human beings! Some of you must know at least one of them! You're just going to sit back and let them die?"

"Sacrifices will have to be made," Hemming says, looking down his nose, "for the good of everyone."

"You're all talking like rescue isn't coming!" Henry exclaims. He looks at us all incredulously. "What about when rescue does come?" Henry wants to know. "What if these people die during the night because we don't take care of them and, when we wake up, there's a helicopter to take us all home?"

"I wanna go home," Alexis whimpers, hands over her ears. No one pays her any attention.

"Then we would have done what we thought was right at the time," Sarah snaps. "For survival."

"This is crazy," I say. I lean down and snatch a bottle of water. When Hemming takes a threatening step toward me, I point it at him aggressively. "Take it from me by force, I dare you. Try it."

The craziest thing is that I can see Hemming and a few others consider it. Really. They look at each other from the corners of their eyes and shift in place.

A warm body comes up beside me and Travis says, "I wouldn't if I were you."

"We give everyone equal resources," Coach Friedman says, authoritatively. He looks between all of us and shakes his head in disgust. "We'll reevaluate in the morning. Until then, no more arguing. And no. More. Fighting." He looks at me specifically when he says not to fight. "Are we clear?"

"Yeah," I say, still in that hard voice. "I got it." I stalk away from them, back to Mr. Wilkins, who looks upset and a little clearer than he was earlier.

"I don't want to make things hard," he says and shakes his head when I offer him water. "I don't need it. You drink it."

"I have my own stash," I say. He accepts it then and even manages to hold the bottle by himself. I feel a little better seeing him able to do it. I curse, calling Hemming something I know Mr. Wilkins won't approve of.

Mr. Wilkins coughs a little. "Language."

I blow some loose hair out of my face. "We're stranded in the desert and you want me to watch my language?" Some of my anger melts away and I feel a reluctant smile tugging at the corners of my mouth. "That's . . . very *you*."

Mr. Wilkins hums and watches the fire, eyes unfocused. I watch the flames with him, ignoring the others settling around on either side of us.

"Pretzels?"

My eyes jerk up to see Henry extending one of those small, blue foil packets to me. "Um, thanks." I take one, make sure that Henry gives Mr. Wilkins one, and then look down at it. My hand is so grimy, covered in dry brown blood and black smears of ash. I wipe them on my pants as best I can but they're not that much better off and don't do much.

"You played so well," Mr. Wilkins says suddenly. He swallows his pretzels with effort and then clears his throat. "I meant to tell you after but . . . I didn't think you wanted to hear it."

The pretzels turn to ash in my mouth. I take a sip of my half bottle of water to wash them down. My throat aches when I say, "I really didn't." *I really don't.*

"You nailed the bridge," Mr. Wilkins says. He's talking about the part that'd taken me weeks to get right half the time. "It was awesome."

I shake my head, staring down at my grimy nails. "But I messed up the timing and I played that other part twice and—"

"You chose a beautiful piece of music," Mr. Wilkins says slowly. "A difficult piece. You played with passion."

"And no technique," I say bitterly. "That's what that one judge said."

"Passion is more important."

"You're wrong," I say. I rub at my eyes even though I'm totally not crying. "If I'd just gotten most of it right then maybe I would have at least placed."

"I am so . . . proud of you," Mr. Wilkins says. When I look at him, startled, he's got a small, fond smile on his kind face. "You make me so proud."

A lead weight drops into my stomach. There's something in Mr. Wilkins's voice that sounds a lot like goodbye. "I don't want to talk about this right now."

"We have to."

"We can talk about it when we get home," I say stubbornly. "Mom and Dad will probably want you to give me extra lessons this week—"

"I'm dying," Mr. Wilkins says, still with that same small smile. "I want to tell you . . . before I go."

"No, you're not!" Heads turn in my direction,

startled by my volume, and I glare at them, especially Hemming, until they turn away. More quietly I say, "You're fine. You'll be fine."

Eventually, the fire gets low and no one wants to get more sagebrush. It's cold now, the temperature falling fast, so we all squish into the shelter, trying to get our body heat to fill the space. I curl up next to Mr. Wilkins like I did last night. This time, with the fire going, it isn't so bad and I feel myself dropping off quickly.

I'm half asleep when Mr. Wilkins's breath hitches. "I wish I could hear you play . . . one more time," he says wistfully. I adjust the blanket so it's over his shoulders and mine but I don't answer. My throat is too tight.

CHAPTER 6

THE FIRST THING I HEAR IN THE MORNING IS yelling. My eyes open the slightest amount and I groan as the faint dawn light hits them. What time is it? Before six, for sure.

"Those fools!"

It sounds like Coach Friedman. What is he angry about so early? I sit up and look blearily around the shelter. I'd only slept in fits and bursts last night so my entire body hurts. There's Max, sleeping, and one of the injured. The guy with the stomach wound is gone though. Everyone else seems to be up already. I frown and look down at Mr. Wilkins. He's still asleep, nostrils barely twitching with each breath. I'm relieved to see even that slight movement. He'd survived the night.

Take that, Sylvia.

"How much did they take?"

That sounded like Henry, voice tight and on the edge of panic. My frown deepens. Who took what? I throw the blanket off and head out of the shelter. I blink in the early morning light and try to make sense of what I'm seeing. I twist around and scan the desert. It's empty all around us.

"Where—where did everyone go?" I ask.

Coach Friedman, Travis, Mrs. Bloomingfield, and Henry whirl around, startled by my sudden appearance. They exchange glances with each other for a long moment, faces serious.

"They left," Henry finally says. "Sylvia, Hemming, Alexis, Sarah—everyone else." He curses and kicks the sand, pacing away aggressively. He stops ten feet from the plane and his shoulders roll. I imagine he's counting to ten.

"Without me," Mrs. Bloomingfield says, distraught. "Why wouldn't they take me with them?"

"They took forty-eight bottles of water," Travis says from where he's crouched by the supplies. Instead of the neat stacks we'd left them in last night, everything is in disarray. "We have twenty-seven left." He looks sick to his stomach. "Split between those remaining—seven—that's less than four bottles each."

"It won't last us more than a day in this heat," Coach Friedman says. "Maybe another twelve hours." He shades his eyes and looks to the horizon. "They won't make it. What were they thinking, leaving in the day? It'll get above a hundred degrees without those clouds, mark my words."

A vicious stab of satisfaction goes through me, immediately followed by self-hatred. I shouldn't be happy that they are going to suffer out there. But a little part of me whispers *forty-eight bottles of water.* With just the six of them, that was eight each. We had less than four between me, Mr. Wilkins, Travis,

Max, Coach Friedman, Mrs. Bloomingfield, Henry and the two injured.

"Hey," I say, "where're the other injured people? The guy with the stomach thing."

Coach Friedman looks bleak. "He died last night. We couldn't leave him in the shelter."

"That . . . " I don't know what to say. "Oh my God."

Travis stands, brushes himself off, and puts a hand on my shoulder. "He never woke up. We don't think he even felt it."

"Where is he?" I ask through numb lips. He'd been on the other side of Mr. Wilkins and he'd died? Just like that? But he'd been alive last night!

"We put him in the plane with the others," Travis says. He slips his hands into his jeans pockets and shrugs uncomfortably. "We didn't want them picking at him."

I shake my head, trying to clear it. "Them?"

Travis opens his mouth and then closes it. Shakes

his head. He takes a hand out of his pocket and points up. I look up and *my* mouth drops open.

High above us, so high that I have to squint to see past the overwhelming blue of the sky, are huge birds, circling. One dives low, coming close enough that I can just make out big, brown wings and a red head.

"Are those . . . ?"

"Vultures?" Travis purses his lips. "Yeah."

I stare at them in horror. Had they smelled the corpses? Sudden images of them swooping down to tear apart the shelter fill my mind. If they couldn't get to the bodies, would they go after the living? Would they go after Mr. Wilkins? No, that was ridiculous. They are scavengers.

"Scavengers," I say out loud, pulling my eyes away from the sky. I have to blink a few times to get the lights out of my eyes. "What else lives around here? That could smell, um, death?"

"Coyotes," Travis says. His brow furrows. "I think that's it? Maybe scorpions?"

"Then it's not safe here anymore," I say. "We can't fight off wild animals." I think for a minute. "Though, if we did, maybe we could eat them." Meat sounds really good right now. I'd woken up with hunger pains and I don't want to ask for food yet. Maybe when Mr. Wilkins gets up.

Coach Friedman barks out a laugh. "That's one way to look at it." After a moment, he sobers. "Dangerous or not, we can't go anywhere during daylight. Dehydration will get us before we even get close to another shelter."

I think about Hemming's group. Was that true for them? I shake off the thought. "So we travel at night." I think about the unending darkness I'd seen last night and shudder. There is no telling what could be hiding out here. "Maybe we should find a light or something."

"Why didn't we just go with them?" Mrs. Bloomingfield asks. She's sitting on one of the suitcases we'd used as seating last night and is fanning herself with one hand. "If we are leaving and taking that risk, why did we wait?"

"You're supposed to stay with the plane for as long as possible," Henry says. He unbuttons his vest, shedding it to be a little cooler. "But if it's not safe to do so . . . that's when you leave."

No one can say it's safe now. The vultures are still circling and the thought of going all day with only about four bottles of water each makes something cold and hard settle in my stomach. I'm so thirsty that my throat aches with it and it's already taking all of my willpower not to chug an entire bottle right now.

"No one managed to do it last night," Coach Friedman says suddenly, "so there's a good chance they didn't do it when they left."

"Do what?" Travis asks, looking up. At some point he changed out of his jersey to a clean, intact shirt. I wonder why I didn't think of that.

"Search the rest of the carry-ons for supplies."

"You mean go back into the wreck," I say. I'm already shaking my head. "I—I can't."

"Neither can I," Mrs. Bloomingfield says quickly, raising her hands as if threatened. "My leg, you know." She gestures to the cut on her thigh. Somehow it looks much better than last night.

"You've done enough, Gloria," Henry says. He looks pale but determined, jaw clenched. "We'll do it."

I feel bad watching the three guys go to the wreck so I turn away before I see them go in. I just can't go back there, not with last night so fresh in my mind. I look at the top of the shelter, where the clothes are piled, and select a clean T-shirt. I don't think any pants but my own will fit me so I just take the shirt and duck back under the raft.

Max is up now and her dark eyes are wide. "Is that true? Did the others really leave?"

I strip off my sweater and shirt, not caring since Mr. Wilkins is still asleep and the injured woman hasn't woken up since the crash. I catch Max up on the plan, though she seems to have heard it all already.

"So, what?" Max asks. "Are the others just going to die out there?"

I pull on my appropriated shirt. It's big on me and the sleeves hit halfway down my arms. I grimace at the fish logo across the front. Well, at least it's clean. "I don't know. They took a lot of water and food so maybe they will find a town or something. Maybe they'll have to stop when it gets too hot."

Max eases up onto her knees and starts folding the blanket she's been using. She doesn't look at me. "I have a cousin who plays soccer in school. In Burbank. He says that they played in a hundred-degree weather once and like half the team passed out. Went all pale and shaky and started slurring and stuff. They called an ambulance and the paramedics said that they were on the verge of heatstroke." She finally does look at me, face drawn. "You can die from heatstroke."

The temperature is already climbing relentlessly

and there's no sign of the clouds today. I swallow. "We'll be fine." I don't sound very convincing.

We lapse into silence and I turn my attention to Mr. Wilkins. There are dark circles under his eyes, darker than before, and he's pale and gaunt-looking. The faint sheen of sweat doesn't help him look any better.

"Mr. Wilkins," I say, shaking his arm. "It's time to get up. Come on, a lot has happened."

All he does is sort of wiggle from the force of my shaking. His head rolls to one side, mouth slipping open. I fumble for his wrist, trying to do what Sylvia had done to find a pulse, placing two fingers about a third of the way across. For a long, heart-stopping moment I can't feel his heartbeat at all. Then, very faintly, I can feel a pulse.

It's really, really weak.

"Coach Friedman!" I roll out of the shelter, ignoring the small twigs and clumps of dirt that get on my clean shirt, and hop up, making for the wreck.

Coach Friedman is just coming out with a

backpack held in his good hand and his bushy eyebrows go way up when he sees me. "Gloria? What's wrong?"

I skid to a halt in front of him, breathing hard. "It's—it's—"

"Hey, you need to stop running," Travis says, worried. He drops the three bags he's carrying onto the ground and peers at me. "You'll run out of steam fast."

"It's Mr. Wilkins," I say, catching my breath. "He won't wake up!"

Coach Friedman limps over to the shelter with me and painfully gets to the ground. He goes right up to Mr. Wilkins and starts poking and prodding at his face and then pats him down. He frowns and looks at Max. "How are you doing, young lady?"

Max starts. "Good. I mean, not good. Um, I'm thirsty and I'm so hungry that my stomach has actually given up growling and my ribs hurt. But, you know. I woke up this morning." She winces and darts a quick look at me. "Ignore me."

Coach Friedman sighs and nods. "Good, good." He runs a hand over the white stubble coming in on his chin.

I can't take it anymore. "Why won't Mr. Wilkins wake up?"

"Oh," Coach Friedman says, eyes flying to mine as if just remembering me. His wrinkles deepen as he frowns. "I'm sorry, Gloria, I know this isn't what you want to hear, but it's very unlikely that Mr. Wilkins will wake up ever again."

I stare at him, uncomprehending. "What?"

He reaches out his good hand, eyes sad and pitying, and lays it on my shoulder. "He hit his head during the crash and I'm afraid that he hit it too hard. He's probably bleeding into his brain."

I fall back onto my butt, away from him. I shake my head. "No, no, he was fine last night! We—we talked about my competition and, and . . ."

"Isn't there anything we can do?" Max asks. "I mean, athletes hit their heads all the time and they don't just . . . not wake up. What can we do?"

I grasp onto this thread, shooting Max a grateful look. "Yeah! There's got to be something!"

"Keep him comfortable," Coach Friedman says. "I'm so sorry but we just don't have the equipment to help him. At least he's not in any pain." He exits the tent, maneuvering to keep all pressure off his left leg while also protecting his arm. I see him go to Travis, who's hovering a few feet away. I see Travis shoot me a horrified look. None of it touches me.

Mr. Wilkins can't *die*. He just *can't*.

I push myself up, body numb, and I nearly tip the shelter over when my shoulders hit the raft. I hear Max's startled shout behind me, but I can barely hear her. I feel like I'm moving underwater. I reach out and spin Coach Friedman around by the shoulder, unmindful of the pained grunt he gives. I'd pulled on his bad arm.

"What if rescue comes soon?" I ask. I feel very distant from what's happening. "They could get him to a hospital, right?"

"Gloria," Coach Friedman says, expression tight.

"I—we just don't know. It's unlikely. He's got hours, maybe less."

"Don't say that!" I take a shaky breath. "If rescue comes, there's a chance he'll make it. He will."

"I'm trying to be honest," Coach Friedman says. "Players I see with those injuries don't have a lot of time without medical attention. In this environment, I'm surprised he's made it this long."

I dodge away from his comforting hand, backing up until I'm out of arm's reach. "He'll be fine." I wipe at my eyes and am distantly horrified to feel wetness on my cheeks. I can't afford to waste water, not in this heat. "I'm going to go look out for a helicopter."

"Gloria," Coach Friedman calls after me but I keep walking.

I go left instead of right, not wanting to talk to either Henry or Travis. I'm cold, even in this heat, and I don't want to see anyone at all. I walk around the wreck, stepping over bits of metal, keeping an eye out for snakes. When I'm confident that no one can see me, I melt down to the ground. I draw my legs up to my chest and fix my gaze on the horizon.

Rescue will come. I know it. It will show up and they'll take Mr. Wilkins to the hospital and he'll be alright. I know he will.

I search the skies for even a glint of a helicopter. High above, the vultures keep circling.

CHAPTER 7

THE SUN IS DIRECTLY OVERHEAD WHEN MAX comes to get me. I hear her approaching and know that I must look ridiculous, sitting on the ground with my arms and legs tucked up inside the shirt. I've pulled the collar a bit over my head in an attempt to keep my already pink skin from burning. I'm desperately thirsty and painfully hungry but I refuse to move from my vigil. Any second now, rescue will be coming, I know it.

"It's me," Max calls. I hear her footsteps come closer. "Thought you might be hungry. And thirsty. Here."

The promise of food and water has my arms shooting out of my sleeves. I accept the offerings from her eagerly and swallow two big gulps of water before forcing myself to set it aside. The pretzels go fast, though—both bags that she's brought me.

"Seen anything?" Max asks. She slides down next to me. She's got a clean top on over her makeshift bandages, and it's long-sleeved.

The curl of fear and panic that I've been trying to ignore rises in my stomach. "No. But that doesn't mean they won't show up." I take another sip of water, letting it wash over my parched tongue and soothe my aching throat.

Max is silent for a long moment, slowly drinking her own water. Finally she says, "It's funny but I should be at my mom's house right now. Watching *Ellen* or whatever while she's out drinking. God, I hate my mom but I wish I was there right now. Or back with my dad. Anywhere but stuck in this desert."

"Oh," I say. What was I supposed to say? What

do you say to someone who's just good as told you that their mom is an alcoholic? "So, um, your parents are divorced?"

"Never married," Max says. "Thought nothing would mess me up as bad as that. Guess I was wrong, huh?" She laughs without humor.

"Yeah," I say. "I guess being in a plane crash takes the cake." I draw a treble clef in the dirt.

"I heard you tell Travis that you were heading home from a competition," Max says. "What type of music do you play?"

"Classical."

Max's eyebrows go way up. "They have competitions for that? Why? I thought you guys just played in a band or something."

"Yeah, competitions suck." I turn my head so I can rest my cheek on my knees. "It used to really get to me but . . . it seems sort of stupid now. I mean, we're in a desert and Mr. Wilkins is hurt and all I can think of is how I flubbed the key change."

"It's your life," Max says. "It's not stupid. I mean,

I'm more upset that my mom's probably called my dad by now than actually being stuck out here. I hate it when they talk. It just makes Dad angry."

I think about my parents. I realize that they know I'm missing right now. They'll be beside themselves with worry, not thinking about how I did at the competition at all. I feel warm because *of course* my parents love me, *of course* they're looking for me. They'd pushed me and pushed me for years but they'd never given up on me. They wouldn't give up now. Heat rises behind my eyes.

"Oh, hey," Max says, alarmed. "Don't cry! That's, like, a waste of water or something. You can't cry! My dad's probably not even that angry, I swear."

"It's not that," I start to explain, wiping at my eyes. "It's just—"

"Max. Gloria."

Both Max and I start, having been too involved in our conversation to hear Travis approach. His eyebrows are drawn low over his eyes and his handsome face is tight with worry.

"Hey, Trav," Max says. "We didn't hear you come up."

"Trav" ignores her, but not to be rude. He's got bad news. "Gloria, Coach Friedman says that you better come say goodbye to Mr. Wilkins. He hasn't got much time left."

The warmth disappears from my stomach and I stumble to my feet. It's been hours and there hasn't been any sign of rescue. I feel like this is another failure. I run back around the plane, making a beeline to the shelter.

Inside, Mr. Wilkins is still and pale. His skin is pressed tight to his skull and the bags under his eyes are even more pronounced than before. He looks, I think, like death itself.

"He just seized," Henry says. His hands are on Mr. Wilkins's head, holding it steady, but they shake in place. "He's fading fast."

"If you've got anything to say," Coach Friedman says from outside the shelter, "now's the time."

My hands flutter around Mr. Wilkins's shoulders.

He looks uncomfortable on the hard ground. "Maybe if we move him—"

"No," Henry says. "I'm sorry, but this is it, Gloria. If I were you, I wouldn't waste any more time denying it. He's only got so long."

I choke on a sob, eyes welling with tears. Seeing him like this . . . They're right. Mr. Wilkins is dying and I'm not helping him by staring into the sun for a chopper that doesn't exist. I feel the dam breaking and the despair I've been holding at bay comes screaming to the surface.

"We'll give you some alone time," Coach Friedman says gently. "Come on, son, let's give them some space." Henry nods and edges out from under the shelter. I peripherally register them walk away but all I can focus on is Mr. Wilkins.

I don't know how long I sit there, staring at him, trying not to waste water by crying. Minutes probably, but it feels like forever. Finally, I take a deep breath and say, "I don't want to say goodbye."

Mr. Wilkins doesn't answer, just lies there with his head at an odd angle and barely breathes.

I sniffle and curl into a ball, hugging my knees to my chest. "I'm not really good with words," I say. "You know that. I don't say what I think ever and I . . . I'd rather just avoid it all. All the time. I don't know what to say. You can't go until I figure out what to say!"

I stop, chest heaving, and close my eyes. My thoughts are all in a mess.

I wish I could hear you play . . . one more time.

Mr. Wilkins had said that last night. His last words to me. My throat tightens and I stand. I may not know what to say but I can do at least one thing for Mr. Wilkins right now.

No one stops me as I make my way to the plane and no one says a word as I walk unhesitatingly into the cabin. The air is still sweet and putrid with the smell of rot but my mind is too numb to react. I go up to my old seat and drop to my knees. My violin case is still wedged in the space meant for carry-ons, a little too long but otherwise safely stowed. I hope there's no damage.

My eyes skip over the dead as I leave, case clenched in one sweaty hand. I go back to the shelter and settle next to Mr. Wilkins. When I open the case, I'm thankful to see that my violin looks unharmed. The hard-shelled case can, apparently, survive a plane crash.

It takes me awhile to get it back into tune, especially since I don't have perfect pitch. Still, I can at least tell where C is supposed to be and I play it against the other notes until it's passable. I prepare my bow and then, in one fluid motion, I bring my instrument up under my chin. I don't have any idea what I'm going to play. I just start.

As I play, I can't help but think everything sounds different. I'm not focusing on the notes right now but instead trying to send the music to Mr. Wilkins.

Mournful and yet grand is the destiny of the artist.

Franz Liszt may have been right. Behind every great musician, composer, and artist is a wall of suffering. It hurts something deep inside to think that this is mine.

I'd rather keep losing competitions.

I draw out a high note, driving the thought away, and dive into something a bit more complex to keep my mind occupied. *Scheherazade* from *The Thousand and One Nights*. My competition piece.

This time, I nail it.

CHAPTER 8

STOP PLAYING WHEN MY TOUGHENED FINGER-tips begin to ache. I feel like I've been in a fugue for hours and, when I look at the position of the sun, I see that I have.

Mr. Wilkins isn't breathing. It's been awhile since I first noticed.

My throat feels raw and swollen and I swallow reflexively. My hands are eerily steady as I pack away my instrument. I lick my dry lips.

"Goodbye, Mr. Wilkins," I say. I reach out and cup his jaw in the palm of my hand. He's empty and I can tell. I withdraw my hand, cradling it against my stomach. "Thank you for everything. And I'm sorry."

I thank him because, while I've been playing, I've realized something. They've only cared about me—Mr. Wilkins, my parents. They've only wanted me to learn and grow. Even if I can't win competitions, I can live. I can survive. I'm going to find a way to keep on living until we're rescued and I can see my parents again. Until then, I can't mourn Mr. Wilkins. I can't break down. I have to keep moving forward.

So I apologize because I'm not going to cry over Mr. Wilkins for a good long while.

I drag my case with me out of the shelter. I see my half-finished water bottle sitting to one side and I grab it, draining it in one go. It's nearly sunset and I need the hydration.

"We're leaving soon then," I say, walking over to where the others are sitting. Henry watches me carefully, probably taking in my red eyes and swollen fingers. Travis and Max are looking at me like they've never seen me before and Mrs. Bloomingfield has pity in her eyes.

Coach Friedman says, "Well, we have to talk about that. Henry, a word?" He stands from the circle and heads to the opposite side of the plane. Henry reluctantly follows.

"You said you weren't any good," Travis says awkwardly. He shrugs his broad shoulders. "You know, on the plane. When I asked you if you could play, you said 'no.'"

"She competes," Max tells him.

"I thought it was lovely," Mrs. Bloomingfield says. "A fine send-off to our dear friend, Mr. Wilson."

"Mr. Wilkins," I correct, voice flat. I spy a bag of pretzels and lick my lips. "May I?"

Max gestures for me to go for it. "What do you think they're talking about?" she asks, jerking her chin to where Henry and Coach Friedman disappeared to. I love her for the subject change, especially since it seems to make both Mrs. Bloomingfield and Travis forget about me instantly.

"I don't know," Travis says. He looks upset to admit it. "All afternoon they've been sneaking away to talk. Coach Friedman hasn't said anything."

I frown. "Maybe they're trying to figure out how to ration the food so we can make it farther tonight. We are still going, yeah?"

"I'm against it," Mrs. Bloomingfield announces suddenly. She's been pretty quiet but now looks down her nose at us. "It's preposterous, what with my injury. Not to mention Henry said we ought to stay with the plane. I think it'd be foolish to abandon it now."

"He said to stay with the plane if it was safe," I say. "You know what comes after vultures? Coyotes. Other scavengers. I don't think it's safe anymore."

"We do need to find a water source," Travis says. "It's hard to notice but we're all already being affected physically and mentally. We're weaker and slower. It'll get worse the longer we have to ration this severely."

"Exactly," Coach Friedman says. He leads a distinctly unhappy Henry back to the circle. He props his good arm on one hip. "The night will help you keep what water you do have as well as keep you out of the sun. You'll leave as soon as the sun goes down."

Travis, Max and I look at each other. Travis slowly raises his head. "'You?'" he asks.

Coach Friedman nods decisively. "You. I won't be going and neither will Mrs. Bloomingfield. We'll hold down the fort here."

Travis launches to his feet. "We should all go! It's dangerous to split up even more than we have!"

"I protest!" Mrs. Bloomingfield exclaims. She quits fanning herself for a moment and tries to catch Coach Friedman's eyes. He doesn't acknowledge her, holding out his hands to Travis.

"Travis," Coach Friedman says, "look at the hills. Those are your best chance for water. Look at how far they are. Both Mrs. Bloomingfield and I are injured. You have to make it to those hills in one night and we'll just slow you down."

"No you won't," Travis protests, eyes sliding to Coach Friedman's broken arm. I bet he's also noticed Coach Friedman's limp is getting worse. Still, he tries. "We need to stick together."

"It's smarter for some people to stay here," Henry says. His arms are folded and he's barely recognizable without his flight attendant uniform. He doesn't look that much older than Travis. "That way, when rescue comes, there'll be someone here to tell them where we're going."

I think that makes sense. If rescue does come, who's to say they'd be able to track us? Maybe it'd be better if someone does stay. I can tell that Travis isn't thinking the same thing.

"I don't like it," Travis says.

"I'm over sixty," Coach Friedman says irritably. "I don't heal like I used to. I've got a broken arm and my left leg's seized up almost completely. I. Will.

Slow. You. Down. And slowed down isn't something y'all can afford to be."

Travis is shaking his head, his face distraught. "What if rescue doesn't come? There's no more water! We can't just leave you like that."

"I'm actually not that injured," Mrs. Bloomingfield says. "More of a flesh wound, really."

"Oh, so you mean that you've just been skipping work," Max says. She rolls her eyes. "What a shocker."

"I was a little injured," Mrs. Bloomingfield says, nose in the air.

"Well, you—"

I tune out the bickering, trying to think. The sun is going to be setting soon and that means we have to get moving. The hills, I know, probably look closer than they actually are. They could be ten miles away, or twenty. We have to be smart about this, with only three bottles of water each and that much distance to cover. And with the cold—plus the animals and bugs that only come out at night—we have to move *fast*.

"He's right," I say. No one listens to me and I say, louder, "He's right!"

"What?" Travis whips his head around and turns on me, incredulous. "What did you say?"

"He's right," I say again. I shuffle, uncomfortable. "Look at the facts. We'll move faster on our own. We could slow down so that they can keep up, but they'll have to stop eventually, and that's something we can't do. The hills are too far."

"By that logic I should just go by myself," Travis says. "I'm a lot stronger than you. Maybe you'll slow me down too."

I don't let his words get to me and raise my chin. "That may be the case but the distance won't kill me. It'll probably kill them."

Travis rears back as if struck. Max whistles a low "Harsh" and Henry's lips press together in a tight line.

Coach Friedman meets my eyes levelly. "She's right." He turns to Travis. "Son, I have a better chance of surviving out here than I do trying to go there. I've got water and I've got food and I've got shelter. I won't waste energy trying to do anything but survive."

"Upon further consideration," Mrs. Bloomingfield says, "I have to agree."

"No one cares," Max snaps at her. She looks to Travis. "Dude, they're making a lot of sense."

"What if we don't find water?" Travis wants to know. He's grasping at straws. "Maybe we should all stay here. If we go out and we don't get to the hills by sunrise, we could all die of heatstroke. Or what if we get there and we still can't find water?"

He's voicing all of our fears. This feels like a last-ditch attempt to survive and none of us want to contemplate what will happen if our gamble fails. At the same time, wasn't it still better to take the chance rather than sitting here, knowing our time will run out?

"Come here, Travis," Coach Friedman says, waving him over. "Let me talk to you in private."

Mrs. Bloomingfield talks about how she thinks it

is for the best, really, and what exactly she's going to say to our rescuers while Coach Friedman leads Travis away to the other side of the plane.

"We'll follow the trail the others left," Henry says. Mrs. Bloomingfield squawks at the interruption but Henry doesn't seem to hear. "They trampled a lot of brush on their way. That way, if we get found first, we can direct the rescue teams to the wreck and to them."

"Maybe we should go the opposite direction," Max says. She scowls. "After they abandoned us, I don't really want to see them again."

Henry is already shaking his head. "No, they played it smart. Went directly west so they could start with the sun at their back, I think. Those hills are the closest."

I look in the direction he's indicating, off the nose end of the plane. The hills do look a little closer over there, but not by much.

"What should we take with us?" I ask. I look

around. There isn't a lot. "The water, I know, and maybe some blankets?"

"We should take some soda cans with us," Henry says. "We can use them for any water we find. Maybe two or three each, a blanket, your portion of the water. The others left one of the first aid kits." He kneels down, rummaging through it. "Band-Aids, gauze, trauma shears . . . it's pretty well-stocked."

Max and I look at each other. I say, "We'll start packing."

I scramble around the camp, gathering clothes and blankets while Max finds the right number of packs. We've got all of them lined up and ready to go when Travis and Coach Friedman reappear, both with red, swollen eyes.

"We're going," Travis croaks.

CHAPTER 9

IHAVE TO LEAVE MY VIOLIN BEHIND. I KNOW I should be more upset about leaving Coach Friedman and Mrs. Bloomingfield behind, leaving Mr. Wilkins behind, but somehow I'm not. I'm not even that upset when they carry Mr. Wilkins into the plane with the other bodies. Instead, the most difficult thing is laying the violin case in the shelter and walking away.

It hurts. I've had the same violin for three years now, having finally switched from a kid's size to a grown-up size. It was big at first, but I'd grown into it after countless hours of playing. With that violin in my hands, I've gone from being a kid to a grown-up, I realize. And now it's being left behind, along with Mr. Wilkins.

We walk single file, Travis taking the lead and Henry at the back. I can tell from the set of Travis's shoulders that he's fighting to not look back. He's got a cane from the wreck that he's using to poke and sweep the ground in front of him. It's important that he focuses on that job so animals can't surprise us.

I'm not so restricted. I glance over my shoulder, past Max and Henry, to see Coach Friedman and the plane fade into the dark.

We don't talk as we walk. I don't think any of us want to break the creepy silence the night has brought. A faint breeze causes the sage to rub together and I tense at the sound.

"It's cold," Max whispers from behind me.

"Put on your sweater," Travis calls back, equally as quiet.

"It's already on."

After that, we don't talk anymore. We stop by unspoken agreement about two hours in, feet aching and tired, to eat a few pretzels and drink some water. The pretzels are running dangerously low and I know we need to find something else to eat soon, especially if we keep up this much activity.

As we move on, there's despair in each of our faces. We all know that this risk we've taken could mean our deaths.

Inanely, I start thinking about the competition. I'd been so nervous stepping onto that stage. The girl before me—an actual prodigy—had played her piece perfectly and I'd already had the thought that I'd lose.

"It'll be awesome," Mr. Wilkins had said. He'd been partially shadowed by the heavy velvet curtains. He'd been smiling—and alive.

I hadn't believed him one bit and had gone on stage and totally messed it up from the beginning, my violin screeching on a basic scale.

The humiliation seems so far away now. Walking

through the desert at night, not sure if I am going to step on a scorpion or worse in the dark, is so far from where I was two days ago. Right now I'm so tired I feel like lead, my skin is burning from the sun, and my mouth is so dry that it's all I can think about sometimes. It's very, very different from the dread I'd felt stepping out onto the stage.

It'll be awesome. I'd thought that he meant performing would be awesome. Only now do I realize that he hadn't meant the competition, but rather my playing. He'd loved how I play violin, loved it like I used to, and I'd never thanked him for that.

We keep walking.

CHAPTER 10

TRAVIS STOPS SUDDENLY AND WITHOUT warning.

"What's wrong?" Henry asks. His voice is scratchy from dehydration and exhaustion. He slumps past Max, who's taken our stop as an invitation to sit, breathing heavily.

Travis points to the ground about twenty feet away. "Look."

The moon is high in the sky at this point, covering the area faintly in silver. I squint in the dim light and can just barely make out an empty water bottle lying on its side.

"What's the problem?" Henry asks. "The other group must have dropped it. We must be close."

"Ugh," says Max in disgust. "Not those jerks."

"No," Travis says. "Did you not notice? For the last hundred feet, their trail has been veering to the right. All the bushes have been stamped down over there." He points.

Henry straightens up with a frown. "Are we not going straight anymore?"

"*We* are," Travis says. He points this time to the peak of a hill that's higher than the others. It's hard to see, but we've gotten a lot closer to it. "I've been taking us straight to that point. They're the ones going off-course. And that's not the only thing they dropped. I saw some cloth a ways back. Might have been a shirt or something."

"What does that mean?" Max asks. She's cradling her side again and, though it's hard to see her in the dark, I think she might be pale. "I mean, did they see something? Maybe they found water."

"That's just it," Travis says. "There's *nothing* over

there. Some hills, yeah, but they're farther than the ones we're heading toward. Why did they change course?"

Henry's lips thin and he stares pensively into the distance. The sky is a navy blue now and I can tell that dawn is only a few hours off. The hills are still a ways ahead, far enough that I know we won't make it before the sun comes up. All we can hope for is that we reach them before it gets too hot.

"Keep going," Henry says finally. "Maybe they saw something, maybe they didn't. We can't take a chance and keep following them. We have to reach those hills."

And pray we find food and water, I think. "But that divides the trail," I say out loud. I resist the urge to lick my cracking lips. They hurt and, though I want to, licking them will only make it worse. "When they try to find us, it'll divide them up."

"It's a chance we have to take," Henry says. He wipes sweat off of his forehead and looks up at the sky. "Come on, keep moving."

After another few minutes of walking, Travis stops again. He turns and I can see the whites of his eyes as he points off to the right. "I think—I think there's a body."

My head jerks to the right. There's just enough light that I can see what I had initially thought was a shadow is, in fact, cloth. Dark cloth about a hundred feet to our right. We all look at each other in horror.

"Sh-should we go check?" Max asks. Her face is an eerie blue in the moonlight. "They could still be alive."

"If they are, what do we do?" I ask. "We don't have any extra resources. We can't carry them." I pause, unsure. "Can we?"

Travis shifts from foot to foot. "We don't know if it's even a person. Maybe it's just a shirt or something. Like before."

Henry steps forward and past us. "There's only one way to find out. Max, stay here so we can stick to our trail. Gloria, Travis, with me."

We approach the shape slowly, carefully searching

the ground for anything that might try to take a bite out of us. The closer we get, the more and more it looks like a body. There are the shoulders, the legs, and then, finally, a tuft of mousy brown hair.

"Oh," I breathe, stopping short. I recognize the shoulders and hair. It's Thin Face.

"'You really think you'll get far on that knee?'" Travis says softly. At our horrified looks, he elaborates. "That's what my coach said, remember? When they were talking about leaving?"

We look at each other uneasily. Here is concrete proof that people died out here—if he was dead. I shake my head. I'm not going to die out here. I'll make sure of it.

"Maybe he has water," I say suddenly. "We—we should search him."

Henry looks disgusted but nods. "You're right. Come on."

Thin Face looks bad close up. His suit jacket is long gone and his shirt is torn and rumpled. His hair is plastered to his skull. He's facing away from us and

Travis is the one who, with a shaking hand, pulls at his shoulder. Thin Face's head lolls grotesquely toward us. I scream.

"What?" Max shouts, sounding alarmed. She doesn't move from where she is but I can hear her shifting restlessly. "What is it?"

Thin Face's face is just . . . gone. His eyes are hollow pits and there are score marks all around them, as if something came and pecked them out. His teeth glitter through holes in his cheeks and his skin is dyed a dark brown with dried blood. I step backwards into a bush and cry out as the branches pull at my clothes.

Travis looks equally sickened. "Oh my God," he says. "Oh my God." He leans over and tries to vomit but can't. There's nothing in his stomach to throw up.

"The vultures," Henry says. His voice shakes almost as much as his hands. He visibly tries to pull himself together. "We, um, we should search him. He probably drank everything but . . . we have to."

"No," Travis says. He doesn't seem conscious of how hard he's shaking his head. "No way. He smells."

"I'll do it," I say. I'm not a kid anymore; I can do this. I grit my teeth and straighten, stepping out of the bush. I suck in air and nod once really fast. "Yep, here I go." I make myself walk over to the body and crouch down next to him. Travis is right, he smells bad. I pull the collar of my shirt up over my nose and breathe through my mouth. It doesn't really help.

I sort of pat along his front, trying not to think about it. His stomach is hard and stiff, rounded in a way that I don't remember it being. I feel straps around his shoulders. "I think he's wearing a pack."

Travis takes a deep breath and comes up next to me, squatting down. He digs his hands under the body without a word. "One, two—OW!"

I jump at his exclamation, pushing the body over in my surprise. Travis is holding his wrist, face twisted with pain.

"Something bit me!" Travis curls around his hand and swears violently.

I hop away, looking to the ground as I do so. Was it a snake? It was so cold I hadn't thought—*there*. A small, brown scorpion skitters away from us, back under Thin Face's body. My heart pounds in my chest. Were there more? Were they deadly?

Henry is making Travis show him when I look away from the body. "It's one entry, I don't think it was a snake. If it's venomous, I can put on a tourniquet—"

"No," Travis yelps. "I could lose my arm—"

"It was a scorpion," I say. I stand and look nervously around my feet. "Small and brown. It's under the body."

"Oh, man," Henry says. He refuses to let go of Travis's hand. "Quit struggling! I won't put a tourniquet on. We need to bandage it though. It's probably not deadly but it could swell. Come on, Max has got the first aid kit." He starts leading Travis back to

Max, who's just a shadowy figure in the dark, peering anxiously at us. "Let's go, Gloria."

I look between them and the body. I can see the pack now, a thin one but there's definitely something in it. "I'll be right there."

Henry doesn't question me, too focused on watching the ground and making sure that Travis doesn't fall. Travis, for his part, has stopped shouting and is instead focusing on cradling his hand as tightly as he can to his chest.

I turn back to the body.

The strap I can see doesn't have any scorpions on it, and neither does the surface of the pack. I wrap my fingers around the strap and pull. It does nothing but jiggle the body and I freeze, eyes scanning for scorpions. When none appear, I take a deep breath. I'm going to have to reach into the pack and pull out the contents. It's not coming off the dead man any time soon.

I do it fast—as if that will keep me from being stung. I unzip the pack—it sounds like thunder in the silence—and plunge my hand in. I imagine each thing I touch is a scorpion or a snake but I force my hand to wrap around them. I pull out an empty bottle and Thin Face's lighter. Then, I pull out two full bottles and a half-empty one.

I shout in triumph, deliriously happy. I leap over the bushes on my way back to Max, heart thundering in my chest.

"Look!" I drop the bottles on the ground by Travis and Henry. "He had water!"

Henry stares at it blankly. "Why would—? Never mind, that's not important right now. I need to use a little to clean out Travis's wound before I wrap it. Any objections?"

My joy dies as I see Travis's face. Both Max and I shake our heads and Henry wastes no time in gently rinsing out the sting site on Travis's hand.

"That's my throwing arm," Travis says. His voice is trembling. "Do you think . . . " He trails off, overcome with an unspoken fear. I realize that he's afraid he won't be able to play football if something happens to his arm. I swallow hard.

"It'll be fine," Henry says. He puts the cap back on the bottle and carefully wraps a strip of blanket around Travis's hand. "People get stung by scorpions all the time and they're fine."

"Yeah," I say, although I have no idea if that's true. "Totally."

Travis breathes evenly and nods. "You're right. Okay, okay." He doesn't sound okay.

Max picks up a full bottle of water.

"It's weird though," she says. She looks scared. "I mean, they took forty-eight bottles, right? That sounds like a lot but it really isn't. If this guy died, they should have taken what he had left. Why didn't they?"

"We can't know why," Henry says. He ties off Travis's bandage and stands. "Maybe he broke off from their group, tried to make it on his own." He hesitates. "Maybe they didn't think of it because they *couldn't* think of it."

I shake my head as if to clear it. "What? What do you mean?"

"It's like my cousin," Max says. She tries to swallow and her throat makes an odd clicking noise when she can't gather enough spit. "He got heatstroke, remember? And he started slurring and saying stupid stuff. Maybe they didn't think to take the water because they couldn't think."

"That's as good a guess as any," Henry says grimly. "They did leave in the morning. Traveling all day in the heat . . . "

"They might not have made it," I say with horror. I look out across the desert as if I might spot their bodies. "They might be out there, dead. Like him."

"We can't know for sure," Henry says. "But it's a possibility."

Max and I look at each other, terrified.

CHAPTER 11

WE HAVE TO KEEP MOVING. THAT'S THE harsh reality. We can't sit in shock and terror forever because the sky is starting to lighten and that means the sun is going to come up. We share a bottle of water, splurging a little on rationing with this unexpected boon.

Then we keep walking.

The sky lightens too fast, going from black to cobalt to navy blue within a half hour. We try to pick up the pace but it's hard. We haven't eaten for a couple hours and haven't slept for almost twenty-four by that point, and I can almost feel my body breaking down.

"Almost there," Henry mutters every once in a while. It's become his mantra. "Almost there."

The sun breaks over the horizon.

"We didn't make it," Max pants. She sounds stunned. "It's too late."

I refuse to think we failed. "If we get there before it gets too hot we'll be okay. We will." I only have a quarter of a bottle of water left. I think I can make it a few more hours after it's gone and, by then, we'll be there. We will. I chug the last of my water and put the bottle into my pack. I tell myself I'm hydrated enough to make it.

I put my head down, focusing on my feet. *We're there*, I think, *we're there, we're there, we're there . . .*

Then, suddenly, we are there. The hills rise up on either side of us and the vegetation grows thicker than it has anywhere else. There are suddenly rock beds and insects. We stop in this little valley between the hills and look at each other blankly.

"There's no water," Travis says, looking around. His brows knit. "How do we . . . how do we find water?"

Max points and we follow the line of her finger to a small flock of birds flying low over the hill. "There are birds. There's got to be water nearby."

"Let's keep moving then," Henry says. His dry lips have cracked and are bleeding. He doesn't seem to notice. "Everyone keep an eye out."

We move more slowly now because of the loose rock under our feet and the incline. I frown. This isn't what I'd thought reaching the hills would be like. For some reason, I'd thought there's just *be* water. Not another expanse of nothing.

I feel tears well in my eyes but I refuse to cry. The next time I cry, it'll be for Mr. Wilkins and that isn't until we're rescued. I swallow my tears and force my legs to carry me up another incline.

"We have to stop soon," Travis says. His voice is tight with pain and he's taken off his sweatshirt. His shirt is drenched in sweat. "We're losing too much water in our sweat."

"Almost there," Henry says. He takes the lead, picking his way over big, sand-colored rocks. "Almost there."

"Wait!" Max says. We turn to look at her and find her peering into one of the natural pockets made by the rocks. "Look! I think it's water!"

We rush over to her, looking into the natural bowl she's found. My heart skips a beat because she's *right*. It's water!

"The rain," Henry says with sudden understanding. "It must be rainwater! It must have rained here last night."

"I saw clouds," I say. With a trembling finger I reach out and touch the water. It's cool though I know it won't be for long.

"There's more!" Travis calls from a little farther up. He's looking all around him. "There are tons of these things—we can probably find more higher!" He scrambles over another rock and then whoops in excitement. "There's a big pool of it up here, in the shade!"

We abandon Max's tiny pocket and go to Travis's. He helps me over a big rock and I stare uncomprehendingly at the water. It's murky, the edges of the pool dark with mud, but it's *water*.

I let Travis lower me down from the rock and fall to my knees. I plunge my hands into the water with a laugh, aware of Max and Travis doing the same thing. We'd made it! I cup my hands, bringing up a palmful of water. I'm about to bring it to my lips when I'm stopped by Henry's shout.

"Wait!" He drops down next to me and shakes my wrist, forcing me to break the seal I've made with my hands so the liquid drops back down. "Don't drink, no one drink!"

Max drops her own handful of water and looks at Henry with moist eyes. "Why not?"

"We have to clean it first," Henry says. "Does that look drinkable to you?"

Travis frowns, face drawn. He clearly wants to

drink but, after a long moment, he nods. "He's right. It's stagnant."

Henry looks just as beat down as the rest of us when he says, "We have to boil it, I think. To make it safe."

Travis nods. "Better safe than sorry. I'll start gathering wood." He walks away slowly, stung arm dangling by his side.

"Whatever," Max says. She looks on the verge of tears. "You lot can do that but I'm going to drink. I'll take that chance."

Henry looks pained. "Max, it's not safe. Dirty water can make you sick."

"I'm not waiting," she says. "I'm not." She leans down and scoops up another palmful of water. There, she pauses, as if daring someone to stop her. Then, carefully, she begins to drink.

I want to follow suit but Henry's earnest face is giving me pause. What if he's right? What if it isn't safe to drink? I come to a decision. "We can wait a little more. I don't want to die of dysentery or whatever." I sound flippant but the words physically pain me to say.

Henry exhales slowly. "Thank you, Gloria."

I look away. "Don't thank me, let's just figure out how to do this."

In the end, we have to clear an area like the night before last for a fire. We're lucky that Henry thought to bring the soda cans because we realize quickly that the plastic bottles will melt quickly.

We use the trauma shears—heavy duty scissors— from the first aid kit to cut the tops off the cans and fill them with water. When I look into them, I have such a strong urge to drink that I have to look away and make myself think of the dirt swirling in it. This is smarter and it won't take that much longer. That's what I tell myself, at least.

The sun is rapidly climbing in the sky and it's way too hot for a fire. Or rather, way too hot for a fire if all we needed was warmth. I grimly take the lighter out of my backpack and bring it to the dry leaves that Travis and Henry have heaped in the center. It takes a few tries but it finally catches.

After the fire really gets going, Henry quickly places the cans on the outskirts of the flame, in a bit of ash that's accumulated. Travis pokes some sticks around them so that they'll catch and hopefully bring more flame around them.

We stare at the finished product and then look to one another.

"How are we going to get them out?" I ask. I don't want to stick my hand into the fire.

Travis uses his left hand to rub his face. "Let me know when you figure that out. I have to go sit down."

Henry and I exchange concerned looks when he goes to sit in the shade of a low tree next to Max. Travis has been moving lethargically, I realize.

"I'll watch the cans," Henry says. He nudges me. "Go see what's wrong."

I run a hand along my pulled-back hair, smoothing it down. Max isn't talking to Travis, instead slowly drinking her muddy water out of a bottle. I head over.

"Hey," I say, settling down in the shade. It feels ten degrees cooler and I welcome the relief. "You're acting kind of weird. What's up?"

Travis's jaw flexes and he avoids looking at me. "What's up? Well, I'm stranded in a desert when I should be getting shown the state-of-the-art gym at the college of my dreams. I'm starving and I got stung by a scorpion. How do you think I'm doing?"

Max turns in surprise, forgetting her own irritation in the face of Travis's poisonous words. She looks at me and I widen my eyes at her.

"Don't be a jerk," Max says. It's hypocritical coming from her but I don't say anything. "We're all stuck in this sucky situation."

"Then why'd she ask?" Travis rubs his right arm with his left. I track the movement.

"I just noticed that you're, um, moving slow," I say. I scratch the back of my neck where a mosquito just bit me. "So I thought maybe something was wrong. More wrong, I mean."

Travis is silent for a long moment. Finally he exhales. "I can't move my arm."

I stare at him. "You can't? Is it from the scorpion?" Concern rushes through me and I summon up enough strength to scoot around to his side. "Can I see?"

Silently, he unwinds his bandage. I hiss in a breath as his red, irritated flesh is exposed. The muscles in his bicep jump, straining his thin T-shirt.

"You're moving your arm," Max says. She's leaned in close.

"I'm not," Travis says. He sniffles and I realize that he's on the verge of tears. "It's doing it on its own. It really, *really* hurts."

"Um," I say, trying to think. It's hard though when it's so hot. "Um, okay. It's swelling so we need to cool it down. Right? Or warm it up?"

"I need to ice it," Travis says. He shakes his head. "We don't have ice."

"No kidding," Max says. "We're in the *desert*."

"We could soak cloth and wrap it," I suggest. I fight down my irritation. It's just from being so worn out and thirsty and scared. "Here, I'll go grab some."

I head to my pack, deciding to sacrifice half my blanket to the cause. It's thin and scratchy but I think it will do the trick. I go back to Henry to ask for the trauma shears to cut the blanket and also check on the status of the water.

"Almost done," Henry says. He holds out a long stick. "I think the best thing to do is poke a can out of the fire. Then maybe use some cloth to carry it to the water so we can cool it."

I nod, impressed with his thinking. I'm having trouble remembering what I'm supposed to be doing and he's planning ahead. "Let me know when you need help."

It takes me a while, but I get the wet blanket to Travis. He still doesn't look like he wants company so I wander away. I look out toward the flat land we've come from and squint. I can't see the plane at all.

"Gloria."

Henry surprises me but I can't give him a reaction to show that. I'm too tired. Henry holds out a plastic bottle, partially filled with foggy water.

"It's been boiled," he says and winces. "It didn't help all that much with the color but hopefully anything we don't want in it is dead. I could use some help feeding the fire; I want to do as much as possible to get us a little better hydrated."

I stare down at the bottle in my hand. It's warm but not hot. I could put it back in the pool to cool it down more but I can't wait. "We're going to make more?" Henry nods and I unscrew the cap, drinking deeply. When I'm done, my thirst is only partly quenched. I wipe my mouth with the back of my hand. "Let's do more."

■ ■ ■

I drink another can of water, bringing me up to about six. It's been a slow afternoon, drinking water in the shade, after the frantic walk across the desert. I feel a little clearer after slowly sipping water for a few hours, but I still hurt all over. The aches from the plane crash are now joined by aching feet and a low burn in my arm and back muscles.

The others look rough. Henry is sitting against a low, drooping tree about ten feet from the fire. He's watching over another round of boiling water and doesn't seem like he's up to doing much else.

Max is curled up on her side in the shade, breathing evenly. I think she's asleep. Travis is flat on his back, his arm propped up on some warm rocks. We're hoping the elevation will help with his swelling.

My stomach churns and I bite my lip. Now that I've got water, the insistent hunger is back sharper than ever.

I read somewhere that humans can go for weeks

without food. I don't know how though. I feel like I'm going to die this second if I don't eat *something*.

I stand and Henry looks up. I see he's got a streak of mud on his face. "I'm going to go see if I can find something to eat."

"Take the cane," Henry says, nodding to Travis's side. "Snakes will be out this time of day."

I nod grimly. "Sure."

Travis doesn't so much as turn his head when I grab the cane. I think I should be more worried but I can't muster up the energy. So many things need to be done and I've done all I can for him.

We're in a dip between two hills. I decide to climb up the ridge to my left. I'm not really planning, just going as far as I can without losing sight of the group while prodding the ground every once in a while to scare off animals.

I come up to a big patch of cactus and grimace. It spans almost the entirety of the ridgetop, making it so that I'll have to go down on one side, walk about thirty feet, and then climb back up flat rocks to get to the top. It'll put me out of sight of the group so I don't want to do it.

I'm about to turn back when I catch sight of a bushel of something red. It's an odd color to see after so many browns and greens, but it's there. I look closer into the cactus patch and can see that the red is part of the cactus. There are little balls of red sitting on top of each flat pad, covered in spikes. I think they must be a type of fruit.

I look down at my feet, indecisive. Would they be safe to eat? Should I chance it? I think of Mr. Wilkins. He always said I should trust in myself, trust in my skills and experience, and try new things. Would that work for this, and not just for a new piece of music?

I see another of the red fruit on the ground and lean down to inspect it. There are obvious marks on this one, as if something had taken a bite of it. My heart starts beating very fast. A rabbit could have left these marks.

As hungry as I am, it's good enough for me.

There's a chance that other animals are eating these cactus fruit and that means they're probably not poisonous. I reach out to grab the nearest fruit and pause.

The spines are a problem. They are fine—finer than needles—and there are clusters of them all over the skin. There's no good place to grab it really. I try using both hands, pinching the sides where the clusters aren't. The skin is smooth and has no purchase so when I try to twist the fruit off the cactus, my fingers slip.

Piercing agony races up my arms and I gasp, jerking my hands away from the fruit. Only the space between my index finger and thumb touched the spines but it feels like there are shards of glass there. My hands shake from the pain, making it hard for me to look at the site. It's very faint, but I can see thin, clear needles embedded in my skin. The flesh around them is already turning red.

It's all too much. I just want to be home, in my bed, with a fully-stocked kitchen. I want Mr.

Wilkins to teach me how to play old Pink Floyd songs and I want a big bowl of pasta salad. Tears well in my eyes and I sink to the ground. All I want is to be *home*. It's been four days and my mom's probably crying and my dad's probably yelling at someone in their efforts to find me.

But what if they don't find me? It's been four days and I haven't even *heard* a helicopter or another plane.

I can't give up hope. I *can't*. If I did, what would Mr. Wilkins say? He'd want me to trust in myself and keep trying. He'd think that would be awesome.

I pull myself to my feet, rubbing my eyes with the sleeves of my shirt. I pause and look down. Maybe if I had something to grab the fruit with, I'd be able to get them off the plant. Then I could take them back to the others and use the trauma shears to cut off the spines.

Grim determination sweeps through me. That could work. That's what I'll do.

Nobody acknowledges me when I come back.

Henry is filling up at the puddle again and Max hasn't moved from underneath her tree. I feel like I'm pushing the spines deeper into my skin as I dig around in my pack for the rest of the blanket. I grit my teeth and grab the fabric. The spines are too short to do any real damage . . . I hope.

I take off, forgetting the cane in my hurry. I climb back up the hill, cursing the heat, and make a beeline to the cactus patch. These fruit won't get the best of me a second time. I loop the blanket around one fruit and twist. It comes off much easier now and I crow triumphantly as I deposit it on the ground beside me. Suddenly the fruit is no longer out of reach or just a part of the plant. It's food, plain and simple, and I *have it*. I stop when I've got twelve red fruit beside me. I haven't gotten a single spine in my skin and I feel victorious. I unfold the blanket and use it to scoop the fruit off the ground, handling it gently so the spikes don't pierce through and get me. I gather the corners until I've got a rough sack filled with cactus fruit.

"Suck it," I tell the plant. I hold the sack away from me and start heading back to the others. I can't wait to see what these will taste like. Should we cook them over the fire? Or just eat them raw like the rabbit must have?

A rattle fills the air and I stop like a deer in headlights. I only now remember the cane that I left by my pack. If I'd remembered it, maybe I would have heard the snake before I was *right on top of it.*

The rattlesnake rises and strikes.

CHAPTER 12

IT'S ONLY THROUGH PURE LUCK THAT IT doesn't get me. The snake is huge, seemingly bigger than the first one I'd seen, and it's *fast*. I can't track its head as it strikes, aiming for my calf with huge fangs, dripping with venom. Reflexively my eyes close and I brace myself for the inevitable.

The sack in my hand jerks and my eyes snap open. To my disbelief, the snake has missed, instead hitting the blanket. Its fangs are tangled in the fabric and its body whips as it struggles to free itself.

I drop the sack, not wanting it to be that close to

my hand. Any second, the snake will be free and it will turn on me again.

I will survive. That's what I'd decided. It's just me here—no audience or judges watching my every move. Just me. I have to do this. I *can* do this.

I reach down and blindly feel for something, anything I can use. My fingers wrap around a large rock and I bring it forward without a thought as to what could be under it. It's hot enough that it burns the skin of my palm but I get a death grip on it. I watch the struggling snake and breathe shakily. It's now or never.

The first time I bring the rock down, I miss. The snake twists out of the way, dragging my impromptu sack open and spilling cactus fruit everywhere. I waste barely a second and bring the rock down again, the full weight of my body behind it.

This time, I don't miss.

I hit the snake's head, afraid that it could turn and bite me if I hit anywhere else. The body thrashes, beating the ground and hitting my hand.

It's big and I think it could leave a bruise. The tail hits my wrist again and then begins to wrap, protesting the way its head is trapped underneath the stone.

With a shriek, I press down as hard as I can on the rock. I hear a small crunch and the snake goes slack. I stay there, chest heaving for a long moment. My hair is almost completely out of its ponytail and I can feel how wide my eyes are.

I don't trust it not to be playing dead. I have to check.

I unwrap its body from around my arm. The scales are smooth and oddly cold in the heat. It's heavier than I expected and makes a solid thump when it hits the ground. I take a fortifying breath and lift the stone.

"Oh," I say out loud, staring. I can't even recognize the diamond-shaped head. It's completely gone, somehow. Well, not somehow. I think I can see skull fragments on the bottom of my weapon.

I drop the rock and sit back heavily on my heels. I . . . fought and killed a rattlesnake. A hysterical giggle rises in my throat. *I fought and killed a rattlesnake.* My eyes fall on my scattered cactus fruit. I found food and now I've killed an animal. Maybe Mr. Wilkins was right.

"I'm going to eat you," I tell the snake's body. I stand up shakily and go about picking up the cactus fruit, being just as careful with the spines as before. The adrenaline is still pumping through my body and my movements are jerky as a result. "And I'm not even going to feel bad about it," I say as I gingerly pick up the heavy body with one hand before picking my way back down the hill.

Henry is setting aside another set of refilled water bottles when I come up to the fire. I drop the sack on the ground in front of him, letting the red fruit spill out.

"We have to cut the spikes off of those," I say. "Some of them had rabbit teeth marks on them and I think that means they're safe to eat."

Henry is staring at me. "Is that . . . did you kill a *snake*?"

My grin resurfaces and I nod proudly. "I sure did."

- - -

Henry makes me sit down in the shade and won't let me help prepare the fruit. Instead, he takes the job for himself, not wanting to bother Max and Travis, who aren't doing well. He says that I'm "over excited" and "hysterical." I really don't think I am.

The world doesn't seem so hostile anymore. I mean, it's still so hot that going more than ten feet makes me lose my breath, my hands hurt from the spikes, and my stomach feels like it's trying to eat itself, but this isn't an endless wasteland without food and water. We found water and I found fruit. I killed a snake. We can survive here. We can.

Henry silently hands me the first fruit, ready to eat. I don't wait to see if anyone else wants any. I've gotten enough for us all. I sink my teeth into the flesh and am surprised by the burst of sweetness that explodes in my mouth. It overwhelms me for a moment. After days of water and dry, vaguely salty pretzels, this is like ambrosia.

"Oh my God," I say, staring at the fruit. The inside is red and wet-looking. It oozes where my teeth bit into it. "This is the best thing I've ever eaten."

Henry takes a bite of his own fruit and groans. "I never liked sweet things before. But I could eat this for the rest of my life."

We devour the small fruit in seconds and, after it's gone, Henry immediately goes back to preparing more. I take a moment to just be happy. There's food making its way down to my stomach, I'm drinking another bottle of earthy water, and I'm sitting in the shade. For once, everything seems to be going okay.

My head whips around at the sound of retching. Max is hunched over a bush, clutching her stomach as she vomits all of the water she drank. She sobs after it's over and dry heaves. There's nothing left in her stomach.

"That's the second time she's thrown up," Henry tells me quietly. He snips a cluster of spines off of another cactus fruit, taking some of the skin with it. "She can't keep anything down."

"Maybe food will settle her stomach," I say. I don't want to lose this new confidence that we can survive, but the sight of Max vomiting is doing just that. "I can take her some cactus fruit?"

Henry nods, making short work of skinning the fruit now that he has a place to grab. "Maybe." He doesn't sound very confident.

The adrenaline high I've been riding ends abruptly. "She'll be okay though, right? I mean we have food and water now." I gesture to the skinned cactus fruit and the bottles he's got lined up in the shade. "We'll be okay."

"We will," Henry says, using the shears to point between us. "We'll be able to last a few more days at least, but them? If Max doesn't stop vomiting, she'll get dehydrated. In this heat, that's a death sentence."

"You said them," I say. I run a finger along the length of the snake just to give my hands something to do. "What about Travis?"

"He's—" Henry says and then breaks off, looking behind me. I turn and raise my eyebrows.

"I'm fine," Travis says, slowly walking up to us. He doesn't look fine. His eyes are glassy and his color is off somehow. His arm is exposed to the air and it's inflamed. It twitches, an involuntary movement, and I recoil.

"Travis," I breathe. "Your arm."

Travis shrugs and goes to sit on the ground, only his knees stop working halfway through. He lands heavily and shrugs. "Doesn't matter. We're never getting out of here."

The way he says it shocks me. He makes it sound like just a fact.

"And," Travis continues, "you know what? I'm glad." He takes the skinned fruit that Henry hands him and stares at it with disbelief. "I won't ever be able to throw a football again. *Whoop!* Bye bye, scholarship. Bye bye, dreams." He takes a vicious bite of the fruit. The red juice runs down his chin.

"That's not true," I say. "We *are* getting out of here. Rescue is coming. We just have to wait."

Travis rolls his eyes. "Yeah? How long? Until this poison works its way up my arm? Or maybe they'll come after Max pukes her guts out. It could be when a rattlesnake finally gets you. Then the paratroopers will come raining down but, oops, no anti-venom."

"He's not himself," Henry says. He's watching Travis with heavy eyes. "It's the heat and the pain."

"I'm being real," Travis says. He shoves the rest of the fruit in his mouth and speaks around it. "The other group didn't make it. We all know it. My coach is probably dead. Her teacher is *actually* dead. Why will we be any different?"

Henry looks down at his lap and doesn't say anything. My head is reeling.

Travis is putting words to thoughts I'd barely

acknowledged. What made us different? Why have we survived while others died from less? Mr. Wilkins wasn't even bleeding when he died. Hemming and Sarah were fit and had plenty of water and they're probably dead. How did we survive on less?

"We're different because we know we can survive," I say. I meet his angry eyes evenly and try not to think about how much bigger he is than me. "I know we can."

Travis stares at me. His chest swells with each breath. "Well, I don't. And even if I did, what would that change? If I get out of here there's nothing waiting for me, thanks to that scorpion. It's better if I just die here. Thanks for the food." He takes another peeled fruit and goes back to his tree. There, he lies down on his side, facing away from us.

"Don't listen to him," Henry says. He's hugging himself, staring at the trauma shears on the ground in front of him. "Hope is all we have left."

I don't answer him. I'd thought that that was enough, but after listening to Travis I'm not so sure.

CHAPTER 13

WE DISTRIBUTE THE REST OF THE FRUIT IN silence. Neither Henry nor I know what to say. What could we say? Max barely blinks at us when we pile her share by her head. She does start to eat it after a minute. I hope she can keep it down.

There's nothing waiting for me. Travis's words are echoing in my head. If his arm stays swollen and paralyzed, the scouts probably won't be as impressed as they were before. What will he do if he doesn't get scouted?

I haven't even really thought of what we'll all do *after* being rescued. I've only been thinking about *getting* rescued. The rest is all a bit hazy. The helicopters would come and we'd get picked up. Maybe we'd get taken to the hospital or, in my secret fantasies, a steak dinner.

But what then?

I realize with a pang that I *miss* playing violin. When I think about bringing my bow to the strings, the usual dread isn't there. Instead, I think about Mr. Wilkins teaching me. I like playing and learning, I just don't like competitions. I don't like trying out for first chair to show that I'm the best violinist in the orchestra.

It doesn't bother me that I'm not the best player. It really doesn't. My parents have always pushed me to be better. Maybe they weren't pushing me to be the best though? Maybe they'd been trying to encourage me to improve and that's it.

I look down at my hands. The places where the cactus fruit stuck me are red, swollen, and painful. My thumb can't touch my forefinger due to the swelling, and a feeling of unease goes through me. If this keeps up or gets infected—and man, does it feel like it's going to get infected—then I can give up the violin. Who needs a violinist who can't even hold a C? No one, that's who.

The thought that I might never play the violin again scares me. I realize what not being able to throw means to Travis. It's the end of doing something you love, something you've trained your whole life to do. But, then again, what does it matter if we don't get rescued?

I swallow and turn the snake, letting the other side cook. Could I survive out here for much longer? Could any of us? Max has caught something from the water and Travis's arm looks worse and worse. I can't be the only one gathering food all the time because Travis is right. Eventually a snake or a scorpion will get me and I'll be just as sick as them.

I shake my head, trying to clear it. But maybe I won't get sick. Maybe Max will keep down this food and Travis's swelling will go down. Nothing's set in stone yet. We've done so much just to stay alive, we can't stop now.

If we stop trying, what else will there be left to do?

I try to think about going back home. It feels out of my reach. I know my parents will be thrilled to have me back but there won't be any more Mr. Wilkins. And at dinner, I probably won't know what to do with that much food. There're so many parts of my life that don't feel like they fit now, not just violin competitions.

I'm different now. I feel different, anyway. The humiliated girl who walked out of that competition is gone. She's been replaced by a woman who's fought and killed a rattlesnake, who's had to forage to survive, and who's laid one of her best friends to rest. A woman who has trusted in herself, taken risks, and succeeded.

I look up as the late afternoon sun is eclipsed. Huge, dark clouds, the ones I'd noticed a ways away earlier, have rolled in. Everything feels instantly cooler but, instead of being relieved, I feel dread. Clouds mean—

"Rain," Henry says. I hadn't noticed him come up. His brow furrows. "We don't have a shelter set up. We forgot a shelter."

I hop up, abandoning my snake in the dirt. "What can we use?" I've already torn up my blanket, like an *idiot*. "Um, maybe we could try and rip off some branches and—"

Henry is already shaking his head. "They're not long enough. Our best bet is to stay under the trees, keep to the bases. It's not good protection but maybe it'll be enough."

Under her tree, Max groans and throws up everything in her stomach. Her vomit is tinged red from the fruit.

CHAPTER 14

I T RAINS. THAT'S THE THING ABOUT BEING stuck out here; we have no control over the heat, the animals, or the weather. All we can do is try to prepare and we've failed miserably. The *first* thing we should have thought of was shelter and we didn't. We've failed.

I huddle against Henry, trying to keep as much of me away from the wet as possible. It doesn't really work. My clothes stick to my skin and it's so uncomfortable I could cry.

The rain passes and comes back once or twice

but, for the most part, stays in a slow, constant drizzle. Our fire sputters and goes out.

The sun goes down, taking its hated heat with it, and I'm *freezing*. Henry shivers next to me, teeth chattering. Our wet clothes don't retain any heat.

"Budge over," Travis says. He's got his good arm around Max, leading her over to us. They've got their blankets held high over their heads. We let them in without comment. We need the extra body heat more than we need the space.

The blankets help for a little while but then they get waterlogged and start dripping heavy streams of water onto our heads. It would have been appreciated in the sun when we had a chance to dry off.

"Sorry," Max says and flies out from under our wet cocoon to vomit again. She's had diarrhea as well and I don't know how there's anything left in her to throw up. I think she must be like a raisin inside—all dried up.

Travis's eyes are still glassy but he seems to have returned to the boy who'd protected me at the crash site. He wraps his good arm around the group, keeping us together as we wait for Max to come back.

It occurs to me that we really might die. After the high of finding food and the uncertainty brought on by Travis's earlier words, it's frightening to realize. We're going to die—not from poison or starvation, but from cold. I won't be able to cry for Mr. Wilkins after all. I won't see Mom and Dad again. I won't play violin again.

I choke back tears and burrow closer to the others. They don't have any more warmth than I do and I pray for Max to come back quickly just for the added body heat.

She doesn't come back.

I peek out from under the blanket toward where she'd headed off to. For a second, what I see doesn't make sense. Was that—had there always been a river there?

Max is hunched over a rock, not seeing the change. She dry heaves again and sobs loud enough that I can hear her over the thunder.

"There's water," I say to Henry and Travis. They both raise their heads enough to blink at me. "Like a stream. Flowing. We need to move."

"S'not," Travis says, nearly unintelligible through the slurring. He squeezes me closer to him, for warmth.

Henry looks, squinting through the rain, which has grown heavier by the second. It's hard to tell in the dark but I think a spasm of fear crosses his face.

"We need to move." He leaps up, ripping himself out of our huddle, and starts trying to pull me up. "It's the hills, I didn't think—we need to move!"

My legs are asleep and I feel like I'm floating when I finally manage to stand. "Why? What's happening? Henry, you're scaring me." *And I'm already scared.*

Henry grabs my shoulders. "Flash flood!" he shouts into my face.

My mind is filled with panicked clarity. The rain is coming down now and we—we're in a valley between the hills. We're in a *ravine*. This is where all the water from farther up is going to come.

I jolt uphill, trampling sagebrush.

My breathing is loud, I can tell, but now I can't hear it over the rumbling thunder and the heavy sound of the rain hitting around us. I look to my left and black yawns out endlessly, rolling down to the flat land. Travis is to my right and, in a bolt of lightning, I can see he looks about as freaked as I am.

Henry and Max are nowhere to be seen.

"Henry!" I scream. "Max!" Lightning flashes again and I catch movement down by the edge of the flow of water. My heart leaps as my eyes catch movement. Henry has gone for Max and is trying to get her up the hill. Max, weak from dehydration and who knows what else, is barely able to keep herself upright.

"They've got to hurry," Travis shouts. There's a sound like thunder and an earthquake and his hand flashes out, wrapped vice-like around my arm. "*No!*"

I spin around to where he's looking and feel my

mind go blank. There's a veritable wall of water tearing up the sagebrush and trees and *everything*.

"Hurry!" I scream down to Henry. My feet are frozen in place. I can't make it down to help and back up in time, I *know* I can't. "Henry! Hurry!"

Henry curses, slipping, and pushes himself back up. He and Max are only ten feet shy of us as the water thunders down to meet them. Henry glances at it, shouts, and heaves Max in front of him as it hits. Travis grabs Max's arm and pulls her onto the top of the hill. For a moment, I think they made it.

As lightning flashes, Henry's eyes meet mine. Then the water surges up and catches his foot. It wipes his legs out from under him and Henry is gone.

CHAPTER 15

THE SUN IS FINALLY COMING UP. I'D LIKE TO say that we stared in shock at where Henry had been until morning, but we didn't. We had to focus on ourselves, and I hate that. I hate that so much. We wrap our arms around each other and shiver and shake as the river swells and bucks, eventually fighting its way back down the hill until it's nothing more than a couple of puddles. The rain peters out and stops.

The sun comes up.

I'm numb, physically and emotionally. My fingers and toes have lost feeling and I think my face must be as red and painful as Max's and Travis's. Max looks the worst of us all.

Everything has been swept away. Our water, the cans, the shears, our blankets . . . Henry. Everything. I didn't even think to grab the snake and I feel an absurd pang of regret. I'd told it I would eat it and I hadn't.

The only thing we can do is walk downhill. There's plenty of water caught in the rocks, fresh from the rain, so we hope it's okay to drink.

My eyes scan the side of the mountain, hoping to spot any of our missing supplies. About three hundred feet down I find, miraculously, a single intact soda can. It's been cleaned of soot by the water and is caught inside a bush. I bound over to it and free it, not caring that the branches scratch my arms.

Travis manages to crack a smile when he sees it. Max doesn't seem to understand what I'm holding. She's worse off after no sleep and the cold. I push away thoughts of what to do after she dies. She's not dead yet.

We stop to rest for a while as the sun keeps climbing in the sky. There's plenty of water now but we're all exhausted. We slump together under one of the low trees. Max passes out for a long time but neither Travis nor I can really get any rest.

"Do you regret not going with the others?" I ask Travis suddenly. I twist the can in my hand so that it catches the sun. "Yesterday? Or was it the day before." I frown.

"Day before," Travis says tiredly. "Why do you ask?"

I let my head fall onto my shoulder so I can look at him. From this angle, all I can see is part of his cheek and one eye. "You were right when you said we'd drag you down. I got you stung." I try to swallow and close my eyes. "I'm sorry about that."

My eyes fly open again as Travis reaches out and grabs my hand with his own. He smiles a little when I look at him, his cheek dimpling. "No one's fault. And, Gloria, you underestimate yourself. There's no team I'd rather be on than yours."

"Oh," I say, and feel like I'd be blushing if I wasn't so tired. "You too." Neither of us lets go and we hold hands for the rest of the afternoon.

When Max wakes up, the sun looks like it's thinking about setting. We have to find somewhere with shelter so we keep moving, looking for a cluster of trees. Anything that could shield us for the night.

We're not really planning where we're going. There are torn-up bushes and trees everywhere, the hill scarred in some places by the debris. On the top of the next hill, I can see a gnarled tree that looks like it's been hit by lightning.

"What's that?" Travis asks. He points with the hand that has been stung.

"Is your arm better?" I ask. I come up to his side and peer at it. It does look less red. "Hey, the swelling is going down! That's great." And it is. Everything else is going wrong but if Travis is getting better, that means we have a chance to survive.

I expect him to be excited by the news but he's still looking straight ahead, eyes wide. "I know, I know, but, Gloria, *look*." He uses his newly recovered arm to push me around until I'm looking straight ahead and about twenty feet down the side of the hill. My heart stops.

I can see Henry's back under the twisted branches of a tree. The river is rushing along a few feet from him, though the water around his feet isn't moving as fast. He's not moving at all and I can't see what state he's in.

"Henry!" We rush over as best we can with Travis practically carrying Max. The place Henry is in is piled up with wet dirt and torn sagebrush. The water is a lot slower around it, forming a natural grotto. We crash down into the area.

Travis leans Max against a clear part of the hill and starts dragging the debris away from Henry. I don't wait, instead wading into the still water to get around the branches. The water is still cold from last night, and the mud pushes into my beat-up sneakers as I claw my way up the steep bank.

Henry is pale, highlighting the deep, purpling

bruises across the right half of his face. His right arm is at an unnatural angle but his face is above water. I hold my hand across his face and wait, every part of me tense.

"He's breathing!" I shout. Tears well up in my eyes and I sob, forgetting my promise not to cry. "Travis, help me get him out of the water, he's breathing!"

"Okay!" Travis shoves the last of the plants away and grabs Henry under his armpits. Henry's heels make grooves in the wet ground. Travis lays him out next to Max and drops to his knees next to him. I join them.

Henry looks bad. There's blood seeping through his shirt and pants, one of his shoes is gone, and his arm is clearly broken. There are cuts in random places, one bisecting his eyebrow and curling up into his hairline.

Travis and I look at each other, unconcealed panic on our faces.

"I have no idea what to do," I say. I run my hands

over my hair and try to breathe. "Do we cover the cuts?"

"Stop the bleeding," Travis agrees. He whips off his own shirt and starts to rip it into strips before I can stop him.

My protest dies on my lips. Henry takes priority right now, but what was Travis going to use to protect his skin from the sun? We were all burned already but the long sleeves help. But what was more important right now? Stopping the bleeding or sun protection?

The answer is obvious so I start helping Travis put pressure on the many, many open wounds. We open Henry's shirt and stop, staring at the roses of bruises blooming along his torso. One of his ribs is moving opposite his breathing. It's broken.

"I don't know what to do," I say again. Mr. Wilkins's face flashes through my mind and I choke back a sob. I hadn't known what to do then either. "What can we do?"

This time, neither Travis nor I have any suggestions. We sit back, staring at Henry.

"We can't support another injured person," I say. "Our supplies are gone. We don't have any extra cloth. What are we going to do?"

"We can't abandon him," Travis says, sounding horrified at the thought. "We already left behind Coach Friedman and that lady."

And Mr. Wilkins.

My anger rises, sharp and fast. "I'm not saying we're going to! But we have to find a way to make it work. How are we going to get him patched up? We don't have any more bandages and I don't know what to do about his arm or ribs. We can't move him and there's no shelter around here. What do we do?"

"We could . . . we could . . . " Travis says and stops. His face twists and I know he's just as out of ideas as I am. "We can't leave him behind."

I think of Mr. Wilkins's body in the plane, in the heat. I say softly, "I know."

We look at each other, helpless.

Max rouses for a moment. "What's that?" Her voice is scratchy and very rough. Her lips are so chapped that they're bleeding.

"What's what?" Travis asks and follows her line of sight. He stops and squints. Straightens. "What *is* that?"

"Clouds," I say. I can't see anything else, just the backside of the clouds that plagued us last night. "What are you—"

A black speck is moving across the sky, over the flat land. At first, I think it's a vulture, heading for us already, as if sensing Henry's impending death. But then, I hear the sound.

Whoompa whoompa whoompa.

"A helicopter," I breathe. My eyes go wide and I blindly seek out Travis's hand, unable to look away. "Is that—?"

"It's a helicopter," Travis confirms. He whoops, bouncing in place and squeezing my hand tightly. "It's rescue!"

"Thank God," Max sobs from behind us. Her

voice is so quiet, we can barely hear her, but she says it with the relief we all feel. "Thank God."

Travis and I are jumping around like idiots, waving our arms and screaming as the helicopter comes closer. We can clearly hear the *whoompa* of the blades going round and round. It turns and begins to head toward us. Its lights flash once, twice, three times.

"They're signaling us!" Travis jumps into the air, fist pumping. "Yes!"

I collapse to my knees next to Henry, grabbing his cold, still hand. "They're coming! You're going to be okay!" Tears well up in my eyes. I've never been this relieved in my life. It's not real, the emotion welling in me—it's too big and powerful. It's as if all of the stress and fear have left me all at once and all that's left is an endless, all-consuming joy.

The helicopter comes to hover above us. I can see orange helmets peeking out over the side. A rope drops down, hitting the ground ten feet in front of us. The most beautiful person I've ever seen in my life, bedecked in a bright orange helmet, warning vest, and climbing harness, drops from the chopper to the ground.

Warm, brown eyes meet mine and they're filled with concern. "Are you okay?"

"We're awesome," I say without thinking. "Just awesome."